Uptown's Princess

A Novel
By

Quiana

Uptown's Princess

Email: AuthorQuiana@gmail.com
Facebook: www.Facebook.com/Author Quiana
Twitter: @AuthorQuiana
Cover Design: Sterling Idokogi
Editor: Muhammad Al-Mahdi

God, you have blessed me with a gift. Not only have I been blessed with a gift, but the courage and faith to go after it. There is no thanks that can be given to express how grateful I truly am. But for what it's worth, thanks.

This has been a wonderful journey. To everyone who has read and supported my novel Fallen, thank you. All of you have gotten me through discouraging moments with all of your positive reviews, emails, Facebook posts, and tweets. I have a new family; and with your love and support our family will continue to grow.

My Psycho Editor, Muhammad Al-Mahdi, boy did you put me through it. I appreciate all of your patience and I am so grateful to have had the opportunity to work with you. This is the beginning of a beautiful relationship, and I can't wait to see what else we can accomplish together, thank you.

Jayla and Jamir, I love you and I believe that everything I do is for US. I pray that you will understand and appreciate that in the future.

QUIANA

"I run my city from South Philly back to UPTOWN!"

The boisterous crowd sang the words to the new Meek Mill hit, making sure to shout out the words *UPTOWN* extra loud. The new Meek Mill song "I'm a Boss", was slowly becoming a city anthem with those very words. Any Philadelphian, no matter what city they were in, was proud to sing the words *"South Philly back to Uptown"*, and let everyone see their city pride and that they were a *boss*.

The drunken crowd danced and bopped around to the song as soon as the beat dropped from the speakers. Even the old heads in the bar, a local term reserved for the mature, two stepped to the music. On this night more than any other, the bar also had in attendance more than its usual share of under aged teens, those who would be heading off to college and didn't want to miss out on their last chance at summer fun.

The two eighteen year olds, Princess and her cousin Kia sang and danced around the bar, with drinks in their hands, as if it were legal. In celebration of their graduation from high school the two girls had been partying all summer. Stumbling around and tipping over with every step, Kia finally took her heels off so she could feel the cool leveled floor inside the drab Stenton Avenue bar.

They were Uptown's very own and proud of it. Everything about them screamed Uptown just as loud as the words to that summer hit. From summers at Finnely's playground, cheerleading for the Bantams and working as shampoo girls at salons on Wadsworth Ave., to fights on Haines street, they were Uptown.

Princess paid for round after round of coconut rum and pineapple juice with her graduation money; they were celebrating their accomplishments. They had finally finished high school and only had the future to look forward to. The two girls continued to dance around the bar song after song, smiling, joking, and flirting with everyone around them. One of the bouncers, Po, and the only reason they were able to get into the bar, had to warn them several times to calm down because they were drawing too much attention, but they didn't care. Kia would be leaving in two weeks and they weren't sure when they would get an opportunity to party with each other again. She would be heading for Howard University, leaving Princess in Philly by herself for the first time.

"That's one right there," Mace said in his friend's ear while trying to speak over the music. He had been watching the two girls interact with the bar's attendees since he stepped in the door. Their personalities appeared to be bubbly and complimented their beauty, just how he liked them.

A chubby blonde suddenly stepped into his line of sight cutting off his view of the two girls. "What you drinking, Daddy?" she asked.

He took one look at the tangled blonde weave attached to her head, her too small stretch denim jeans that did nothing for her figure, and the roll of fat overlapping her waistline, and said, "Nah, I'm good, Ma, but thanks."

His appetite was for young and tight skin to rub against his sculpted frame for the night. The woman could do nothing more than be a quick dick suck if his efforts with the other girls failed. He turned his attention away from the chubby blonde and continued to follow the crowd watching the two girls.

The chubby blonde, refusing to be ignored, pressed her fat fingers against the crotch of his jeans. "Well tell me what I can do?" she asked.

Annoyed by her forwardness, but not wanting to cause a scene, he grabbed her wrist and removed her hand from his crotch. With a glare of the eyes, he warned the woman to leave him alone and refocused his attention on the young women he had been watching.

From behind her Princess heard a smooth baritone voice say into her ear, "Where y'all from, beautiful?"

Princess knew she was gorgeous. It wasn't only her sun bronzed reddish brown skin, bright smile, full, pink lips and jet black, shoulder length, perfectly trimmed hair that caught men's eyes. But at 5'7 she had the full package and loved to show it off. Tonight she'd worn a tight pink spandex mini-skirt that accentuated the lean curves of her hips and thighs, and the black Cami top she wore showed off her firm eighteen year old breast to a T. So, she wasn't at all surprised when the man behind her took his time to admire her beauty.

She turned to see who the bold stranger was and was pleased to find a 6'ft., light brown skinned, clean cut, handsome man smiling at her. The YSL t-shirt and dark denim True Religion jeans he wore were a subtle statement that he had style and he didn't mind paying for it.

"Uptown," she said and smiled back.

He laughed. "Mmm, y'all sweet in Uptown, huh?"

Kia, standing behind Princess, cleared her throat loudly and said, "Not that sweet."

The stranger gestured with his hands in front of him that he meant no harm. Kia stared at the man waiting for him to step off. Princess was amused at the standoff between her cousin and the handsome stranger. But before the situation could go any further, she said, "That's my cousin, Kia."

"Okay, cousin Kia," he said acknowledging her, "I'm Mace," then turning to Princess, asked "and you are?"

"Princess."

"Princess. Uptown's Princess; huh? Well you look more like a queen."

Princess blushed, from the corner of her eye she could see Kia rolling her eyes. She ignored her cousin's less than friendly response to Mace. He was charismatic and fly, and he had jewelry to match his stunning appeal. The earring in his ear, the bracelet on his right hand and the expensive watch on his left glistened in the dim bar lighting. She tried to read the brand of the watch but couldn't in the hazy lighting, but she could tell it wasn't cheap.

"Yup, Uptown's Princess. Where you from?"

"All over."

"What you mean all over?"

"I travel a lot. But I'm originally from Southwest."

Princess nodded her head considering the rumors that she heard about the dudes from Southwest and the drug game. She was interested in him. Kia continued to play watchdog over her, but that didn't stop Princess from talking to Mace.

"So why are you here? Southwest is on the other side of town."

"I gotta stay in one place?" He laughed. "My peoples from around this way, so I came to pay them a visit."

He pointed to a few men standing by the door and waved one of them over. A very tall, thin, dark skinned man made his way over to the circle and began distracting Kia from their conversation.

"How old are you?" Mace asked.

"I'm eighteen," she said proudly.

"Oh you just a baby. I wanted to buy you a drink but you're not even old enough yet."

"I am old enough. I've been drinking all night." She said, feeling insulted and not wanting to appear too young to gain his interest.

"Oh yea? You grown— and fancy I see." They both giggled as he took her hand and she let him spin her around to get a better view of her goodies. She was pleased when she noticed the bulge formed at the front of his pants.

"How old are you?"

"30. Is that too old?"

Usually, she would've said yes, but when he spun her around she'd noticed the wad of cash imprinted in his pocket as his shirt rose up. She didn't have a problem with making an exception this time.

"Nope, let's drink."

Princess and Mace walked to the bar. Princess, already drunk, didn't need another drink. Still she ordered another long island iced tea just to blend in. Mace, who didn't appear to be drunk at all, ordered a rum and coke and held it in his hand barely taking any sips.

The two hit it off dancing and joking. By the time the bar closed, Princess was holding onto Mace's arm hot and exhausted from all of the grinding they did on the dance floor. Her silky straight hair had transformed into frizzy waves and her makeup had been sweated out so much that she looked like she had just left the gym.

Mace was a complete gentleman. He walked Princess to her car where Kia was waiting at the wheel. Princess gave him her number and begged him to call her before the night was over. Mace promised he would and told Kia to make sure that Princess got home safe. With that the cousin's headed to their homes which were a few blocks away.

Princess, pressing her head against the car's window and trying to cool off in the icy air blowing out of the AC, blurted out, "I like him."

"You don't even know him."

"But I like him and I'm going to get to know him. That man was sexy. I'm trying to see him again, soon."

The two laughed at her boldness but Princess meant every word of it. She hoped to receive the phone call from him that she requested so that she could get more of his time. Kia dropped Princess off at her home on Mt. Airy Avenue and waited for Princess to fiddle with the house keys and get inside then pulled off. Princess would have to walk over the next day to pick up her vehicle.

Before Princess finished heating up the leftover fried chicken her mother made earlier that night, her phone rang, breaking the kitchen's silence and startling her. It was Mace.

The last thing she needed was for her parents to see her drunk at 2 AM. Her mother frowned upon underage drinking and would nag her about it until her ears fell off. She quickly answered the phone to avoid the loud ringer from waking her sleeping parents.

"Hello."

"Princess, it's Mace babe."

Hearing those words melted her heart. She loved the way her name sounded when he said it and having the word *babe* following it made it even sweeter.

"Hey, Mace, I knew it was you, wouldn't no one else be calling my phone at this time of the night. Where are you?"

"Damn, you sound so beautiful over the phone. If I didn't already know how pretty you are then your voice would give it away. I'm at my people's house about to head back Southwest, I just wanted to make sure you got in safe."

Princess blushed at all of his compliments. She knew she was a beautiful girl, but it was nothing like hearing it from the one you wanted to hear it from. She also knew some of it was game, but she liked playing.

"How about you let me come pick you up and take you home with me tonight?" Mace said.

Though Princess had desired to see him again soon, she hadn't intended on it being tonight and definitely not all the way in Southwest. "Mace it's two in the morning."

"Who said our night had to end so early."

His voice sounded so sexy over the phone. She hoped he wouldn't ask again. His offer, though outrageous, was tempting. Was she making a mistake by turning down his offer? No, she was Princess, not just some booty call.

"I don't know about going to Southwest tonight. We just met, and I barely know you."

12

The line went silent. She hoped his silence didn't mean he thought she was playing games with him, or worse, that she was acting like a little girl. She was definitely not some little girl, and to prove that she wasn't, she blurted out, "You should stop by just for a second. I'll come outside." Her eagerness shined through the phone arousing his intentions.

"I don't want to get you in trouble." He laughed "Your daddy's not going to come outside with his gun is he?"

"I'm grown, come over here so I can see you."

Princess gave him her address and he agreed to come. She was so excited about seeing him that she forgot all about her food and rushed to the basement bathroom to fix her hair and makeup. She brushed her wavy hair into a tight bun, rinsed her face off and touched up her makeup. She knew that men loved her in bright pink lip gloss and that Mace would also.

Carefully, she opened her back door, slipped out of the house and tried not to make too much noise with the clacking of her heels. She Cut down the back driveway and through the grass on the side of her house, then sat on the steps and waited for Mace to pull up.

About 10 minutes later a 2010 silver Lexus GX truck stopped in front of Princess. The truck was crystal clean without a mark in sight. The obscure tint prevented her from seeing his good looks from the outside of the car. Not sure whether to wait for him to step out or to get in the car, Princess sat on the steps and waited for a signal. When she received no signal, she realized that he must've wanted her to get in, she stood up and attempted to open the passenger's side door, but it was locked. Mace rolled the window down and leaned over just enough to be at eye level with her.

"What took you so long to come up to the car?"

"I thought you would've gotten out."

"Nah, get in."

The clicking of the lock permitted her to open the car door without hesitation. The cream leather on the inside of the car was just as clean as the spotless exterior. Perfectly vacuumed, no dust or lint, the car looked as if it was brand new.

"Is this your car?" she asked obviously impressed.

"Whose car would it be?" He laughed, at her innocence, and when he did she felt like a country bumpkin fresh to New York City.

She rolled her eyes at his sarcasm and at her own simple question. "I don't know, it could be a rental. It just looks so new."

"You know people catch eyes when you roll them." She laughed at his joke not fully understanding what he meant. His thuggish presence was strong and not to be taken lightly.

"This is my car," he said. "You just never dealt with a nigga like me. I like nice things and I like to keep them nice. I'm sure you like nice things too."

She nodded her head in agreement remembering the designer tags in her closet waiting to be popped. She liked nice things for sure and liked even more when someone

14

else would pay for them. She was hoping he would be that type.

"So what's up," Princess said, "where are you staying tonight?"

"Well I can't stay with you. I'm going back to Southwest, just wanted to see your pretty face before I head to Miami."

"Miami! Awww man, I wish I could go to Miami! Everyone is leaving but me."

"Who's everyone?"

"Oh, my cousin Kia is leaving for college in two weeks"

"Yea? And what will you be doing?"

"Looking for a job, chillen, you know." Ashamed of her less than respectable answer, Princess fixed her eyes in her lap.

"Well don't worry; I'll be back in two weeks. Some friends and I gotta handle some business, but then I'm coming right back. Have you ever been to Miami?"

She shook her head no. "Alright," Mace said, "we gotta get you down there."

Princess smiled at his statement. Mace had a presence about him that was powerful. When he talked, it was more like giving orders, not just words coming out of his mouth. She liked that about him. His tone was commanding and made her want to listen. His eyes had a spark that set off with a fiery essence when he looked at her. She thought she was seeing things but somehow when he spoke, that spark would fly and it was almost like he was hypnotizing her.

The cool air from the AC chilled her rising temperature from the alcohol and helped Princess to relax. She fixed the seat and laid back. Mace listened to how she had just graduated but didn't have a real plans for life, and how she wasn't sure if she wanted to go to college. Princess babbled on about not wanting to work a low paying job until she decided on her plans and how her daddy usually made up for her losses.

Without warning Mace grabbed her breast. Before she could stop him, he kissed her lips, silencing her protest. Princess felt every bit of his kiss and melted into it. Mace squeezed her breast harder between his long thick fingers, groping them like a ball of dough. Then he slid the spaghetti straps from her shoulders until her brown juicy melons were exposed. Moving his tongue from her mouth to her nipple, he used his soft lips to grip it with the right amount of pressure.

Princess let out moans of pleasure as she shifted her body deeper into her seat. A burst of juice flowed from her vagina as Mace used his fingers to tightly grip her hardened clit. Roughly holding her pussy tight and shaking his palms on her clit, Mace cupped his lips around her nipples evenly attending to both. His mouth was warm and not too wet. He sucked and licked on her breast better than anyone had ever done before. She was never a fan of getting them licked, but now he was showing her why people bragged about getting it done. The wetness of his tongue mixed with the cool air made her legs spread hoping he would submerge into her aching walls. The alcohol no doubt enhanced her feelings and made her anxious. She dripped onto her skirt as stickiness flowed between his closed fingers.

Mace undid his pants until his dick was hanging out as long and thick as she guessed it would be. Mace leaned his seat. Princess looked at him unsure about giving him head. She had only done it a few times but never to a penis that big. Mace was built like a horse and she didn't want to embarrass herself and choke. She started to lean down and hesitated.

"Don't be shy *now*," he said. He then grabbed the back of her head and guided her face down to his pulsing penis.

Princess, turned on by his baritone voice and not wanting to seem like an amateur, went to work on the head of his penis. Her soft cushioned lips formed the perfect pillow for his penis as she cupped her lips over her teeth. His length reached the back of her throat without effort, making it hard for her not to gag as she struggled to take all of Mace's width in. She bobbed up and down to her own rhythm never stopping for air, allowing the saliva in her mouth to grow as she became more proud of her tongue game. Globs of spit poured off her tongue and Mace used his hips to push his hard penis further into her mouth until she gagged.

"Good Princess," he said, "just like that, good girl." He would say urging her to keep at it.

Princess tried her best to show him that she could handle her own. Using her hand as a compliment to her deep slurping, she was out to prove that she was daddy's big girl. He continued to fling his pelvis up and down while pushing down on her head. Mace rubbed her bent over ass while she sucked on him. He then slipped her panties to the side, slowly inserted first one, then two, then three of his thick fingers inside of her soaking wet vagina, and began rapidly stoking his fingers in and out of her. His penis thickened in her mouth and she knew he was close to coming. The truck was getting hot, she couldn't breathe with all of the pressure being applied to her vagina and mouth. She propped her ass higher into the air to let his fingers dig deeper. Suddenly, he snatched her head from out of his lap and told her to turn around. Still off balance, she changed positions and bent her body over the front seat.

"But my parents might see us."

"Shut up, can't nobody see in this car." His aggression washed away her argument.

She spread her bare ass over the reclined seats as he hunched over her body. Not wanting a condom to destroy the feeling, she inserted him into her pussy and gasped when he pounded his body against hers. Her soft cheeks jiggled with every stroke as she cried out at the pleasure.

"Oh my God!" Princess screamed, and Mace ripped her insides apart even more. Their first encounter was turning out to be an exhilarating experience.

"So fucking tight," he said. Mace grunted into her ear as she clinched his penis between the walls of her vagina. He was so big that she wasn't sure if it was pleasure or pain, but she knew she was enjoying it. He had the biggest dick she had ever encountered, and her tight vagina was not used to someone with such girth. Mace dug deep into her stomach with strong fast strokes. She tried to match his strokes but found that she couldn't. He was too big, his strokes too powerful, and before long, he was completely dominating her. Mace pinned her face into the leather headrest so that she couldn't move, and then she felt him change his stroke to a slow, pounding grind. She was enjoying the sex more than she imagined she would. Mace was so experienced, and she was soon lost in the powerful rhythm of his stroke. After tonight, she knew she would never be able to get enough. He moaned and groaned with each stroke until he erupted and shot hot come all over her ass.

Mace grabbed a towel from under the seat and told her to clean herself off before sitting down. She wiped her body off hoping that the rag was clean, then fixed her clothes.

"I'll be back in two weeks for you," Mace said, "and I'm going to have a surprise."

"A surprise?"

"Yup, pussy that good deserves to be taken care of, it should be famous." They laughed.

"I gotta go."

QUIANA

The sun was coming up and she knew that her mom would be waking soon. She had to sneak back into the house, undress, and get in the bed without her parents noticing. She was embarrassed enough, so, she was glad Mace didn't ask any questions that would require an explanation. He gave her one more kiss and she quietly exited the car and scurried back into her home.

"Whatever happened to that guy Mace that you met at the bar?" Kia asked.

"I fucked him," Princess said, never taking her eyes from the moving van parked out front. Beads of sweat trickled down the sides of her face from sitting in the sun, but Princess barely noticed. Her eyes followed the loading of the van that would take Kia to school, an otherwise happy event overshadowed by the fact that Kia would be leaving.

"When?" Kia asked. She threw a playful jab at Princess's arm. "Why didn't you tell me?" Kia's antics weren't the least bit entertaining to Princess. She pouted and crossed arms over her bent knees.

"That same night," Princess said. "I didn't tell you because I didn't know what you were going to say. It was good too, great."

Kia frowned. "So now you're afraid of what I might say? You already know I'm no angel either, and I never hold back on you. So, what's up wit y'all?"

"He's in Miami and should be back tomorrow." Secretly she wondered whether she would see Mace again. At that thought her vagina instantly grew moist.

"Have you spoke to him since?" Kia asked.

"No," Princess said. The more they talked about Mace, the more vivid the events of the encounter with him grew in her mind.

"Well he'll probably call you when he gets back," Kia said. She looked over at the moving van then stood. "You ready for this?"

Not wanting to cry, Princess nodded her head and held back the tears that threatened to fall at any moment. Princess stood too, and the two girls walked towards Kia's moving van. Princess tried to be happy for Kia, but even thoughts of visiting Kia on campus and getting the scoop on being in college could not replace the sense of abandonment Princess now felt. She had never been away from Kia for longer than a week, and now they wouldn't see each other for at least two months.

Other than Kia Princess didn't really have any friends. She had a hard time relating to other females and didn't trust that they would ride for her like her cousin would anyway. She was really going to miss her cousin.

"Don't look so sad," Kia said. "You know all you gotta do is call right? If you need advice or someone to talk to, all you have to do is call. The angel on your shoulder will still be there to answer." She smirked, and Princess returned Kia's smile with a half grin she hoped her cousin couldn't see right through.

Kia was only going to college, but it meant a lot of changes. Kia would be making new friends and gaining new experiences. They would always be family, but after Kia went away what would they have to talk about?

"I'm serious," Kia said. "Don't be too proud to call."

"I won't," Princess said. "You just make sure you find me a cutie to hang out with when I come to visit you on campus." Princess bumped her hip against Kia's, causing her cousin to stumble and lose her balance.

They hugged and kissed each other, and then Kia crammed herself into the back of the moving van with all her belongings and slid the door shut.

Princess arrived at her home and focused her mind on hitting the bed. She had absolutely no plans for the evening and no one to look forward to giving her time to. Her parents nagged at her to fill out applications to find a job but she wasn't in any rush. Besides, no jobs that she could apply to would pay much anyway, and she knew her father would give her what she needed.

Locking the door, Princess secluded herself within the confines of her bedroom. Looking around the room thoughts of remodeling pranced in her head. *Grow up Princess.* She swept a disapproving look over the room's décor and sighed deeply. Everything about the room was juvenile. Stuffed animals sat on shelves that were nailed into her hot pink walls, and pictures of high school friends and her celeb crushes still covered the headboard of her full size bed which was padded in pink and black zebra sheets.

Princess placed a towel underneath her door and lit a roach from a blunt she had smoked the night before. She refrained from calling Kia, knowing they needed time apart. She scrolled through her phone and attempted to find a possible date for the night, but her prospects looked bleak. A meal of Mace would be the best dinner tonight, and none of the rowdy, barely 21 year old men in her phone would even come close to him. The only person she could think to call was her ex-boyfriend T.

Even after their breakup, T was the closest thing that she had to a man. They still had astonishing sex, and he still referred to her as his girl, but she knew he had lots of women. That was the reason why they had broken up. The truth was Princess secretly liked the drama. When they weren't together, the men she met were boring. Guys who catered to her and aimed to be by her side couldn't keep her attention. She couldn't stand their constant pleas to be in a relationship. She knew for most of them, she was nothing more than a bragging right amongst friends in the competition to see who could get the baddest chick. T didn't treat her like that.

T treated her like the average female on the street, and she liked that about him. He would tell her over and over again that pretty girls come a dime a dozen, and good looks fade overtime like a pair of dark denim jeans in the washer. He didn't put her on a pedestal, in fact, she found herself trying her best to keep his attention and to keep up with him. Fly clothes, new hair styles, high heels, she tried everything she could to keep his focus on her.

"What you doing tonight, T?" Princess moaned, hoping he would give her the answer that would save her night.

"I'm busy," he said.

Princess noticed his abrupt tone but needed a distraction from her own loneliness. "Too busy for me?" she asked.

"Yea, tonight I am. I got some runs to make. You can come by later when I'm done though."

She knew what those words meant and scrunched up her face because of the insult of his suggestion. Sex was on her mind, but it was his job to make her feel like more than a quick, late-night booty call.

"Kia went off to school," Princess said.

"So what you lonely?"

"Yea, and I'm high as a kite," she said. "Can I see you?" That little hint should've been the kicker for a *yes*. She waited for his answer like a frisky kitten anticipating play.

"Nah, I got shit to do. But like I said, you can come by later."

"Fuck you, T." She hung up the phone in disgust. He had no respect for her or for what they had. A catalogue of names and faces of girls that T was known to have had relations with raced around her mind. *Which bitch was he fucking tonight?* Angry at herself for feeling jealous, she suppressed thoughts of a surprise visit to T's. She skimmed through her phone book one more time in search of a savior with no luck.

A half hour later T called, putting a smile on her face, and warning her body to prepare for pleasure. As hard as he tried, she knew he couldn't resist her.

"C'mon over," T said, "I still gotta run out, but you can chill here til I get back."

He wouldn't be going anywhere. She intended to use her succulent pussy as a trap to keep him by her side for the night. Once she was in the apartment and they fucked, all it would take was a nap and some food for him to forget about his plans. T's intentions were always sick but she had the remedy.

Princess put together her overnight bag, then put on a pair of booty shorts and a tight T-shirt. The cup of her cheeks showed every time she moved in the little shorts and would catch anyone's attention. She didn't even bother to put a bra on underneath her shirt since she would be going directly over to T's.

When she arrived at T's small apartment in Germantown, T was high from marijuana and wearing nothing but a pair of boxers. He didn't ask about her day or even allow her to put her bag down before he roughly groped her ass and started kissing her neck.

"Damn, babe, can I get a hi?" Princess said. She tried to push him back, wanting to feed her need for foreplay, but T wouldn't let her go.

"Ain't this what you wanted?" he asked.

He kissed her some more until she gave in. T pulled down his thigh hugging red boxer briefs to his ankles and flopped on the couch. *Damn this boy is sexy!* His penis was hard and standing straight up. He looked up at her, eyes low and his legs spread apart, giving her the perfect view. She couldn't deny his good looks: 6'1", slim built with strict muscle tone, deep waves that created a typhoon in his hair, and an impeccable smile that served to increase his boyish charm. Carefully crafted tattoos covered his chest and both of his long lean arms. His body screamed *thug*. She had been with him during the process of him getting his arms completely inked, and they were enticing to her. Seductive and street, his tatted body spurred her into a hood fantasy every time he dug inside her.

Princess knew the routine. He was waiting for her to get on top and ride him. She loved how he ordered her around during sex. So bossy yet so silent, his controlling ways made sex exciting. She unbuttoned her shorts and slid them from her hips. Cuffing her wet panties to make sure she was ready, Princess waited for permission to mount his curvy banana stick. She slid her wet panties to her ankles leaving her sticky hot box face to face with T's moistened lips. The steamy night with Mace in the car suddenly sprang to memory and formed a twinge of guilt in her stomach. She didn't use a condom with him that night and the thought made her feel uncomfortable and scared at the same time. If he had anything and she gave it to T, T would beat her ass for sure. Not only that, but she felt dirty fucking another man without a condom in such a short amount of time.

Princess knew the question would rang an alarm in his head, but she asked anyway. "T, you got a condom?"

"Condom?" T frowned and his dick began to shrink. "A condom for what?"

"Because I don't know who you've been fuckin?" she said quickly, trying to keep the focus off herself.

"I ain't fuck nobody without a condom," T said. "Who the fuck you been fuckin?"

This muthafucker. She was furious that he didn't try to cover up that he was having sex with other females. As bad as she wanted to have sex with him, she didn't want to do it without a condom. If he wouldn't use one, which he should've had since he did say that he was using them, she would just have to go home with a wet pussy.

"Well if you use one with other bitches then why can't you use one with me?"

"Who you been fuckin Princess? We ain't never use no condoms, so why we gotta start now? You been fuckin somebody, huh?" Arms tucked across his chest, T leaned forward, forcing eye contact from Princess.

"I ain't fuck nobody." Her lie fell on deaf ears. He jumped to his feet and brushed past her. Princess stumbled backwards and caught her balance. "Why you get up?" she said, watching him tuck his now limp penis into his boxers and saunter to the bedroom.

"Bitch, get the fuck out. Comin' over here with that dumb shit."

28

T slammed the bedroom door leaving Princess in the room alone. She was now forced to consider whether she really wanted to stick with her decision to go home with her vagina dripping wet. She heard T shuffling around in his drawers, probably looking for clothes to wear to another woman's house, so that meant she had better decide quickly.

When T came out of the bedroom she stood waiting for him naked, in the middle of the living room floor. She knew she had made the right decision when T, without hesitation, dropped his pants to his ankles, pulled his dick through his boxers, and bent Princess over the back of the sofa.

The sex was good but her mind was occupied by thought's of Mace. Mace's dick was bigger, a grown man's dick, and she wondered if he stretched her out a bit. She hoped that T couldn't notice a difference.

Princess woke up in T's queen sized bed to a pitch black silent house. He wasn't anywhere in sight and never woke her up to tell her he was leaving. It was 12 AM, so she really had no clue where he was. She picked up her phone to call T, and paused when she noticed the missed call from Mace. Princess wished he'd called a few hours earlier so that he would've been the one she fucked, but she was still ecstatic to see the call. Cautious because of whose house she was in, she took a walk through the apartment before calling Mace back. A quick sweep and just as she suspected, T was nowhere to be found. She called Mace.

"Hello?" The sound of his voice soothed her. She hadn't heard from him in two weeks and had thought about seeing him the whole time.

"Hey, it's Princess." She tried not to sound too excited but she couldn't help herself.

Mace as always was calm and cool. "Hey, love, I'm back."

"How was Miami?"

"The water was warm and blue, the weather was perfect, paradise in the United States. Only one thing was wrong with my trip."

"What was that?"

"You weren't there. Can I see you tonight? You can come over to my place," he said.

"I'd love to, Mace, but I have to let you know that my period is on."

He laughed. "We don't have to have sex every time we see each other."

"That's an answer I'm not used to hearing. Most men get mad if you come over during that time of the month."

"I told you before I'm a different type of nigga. Take down my address, I'll see you when you get here."

Princess sent T a short text informing him that she was going back home. She then showered, and dressed, and left her crusted panties in T's dirty clothes hamper. If another woman was doing his laundry, she would be in for a surprise. She also decided to leave her overnight bag at the foot of the bed in case he decided to bring someone back to his crib after a night out. The big Victoria's Secret logo would raise an eyebrow on any female's face.

Southwest was on the opposite end of the city. Princess was unfamiliar with anything below Center city. Uptown and North Philly, Princess pretty much stayed in her neck of the woods.

The city was hotter than ever, and the sticky August humidity was suffocating. The broken air conditioner in Princess's car didn't help. A flushed glow left her looking sweaty after her thirty minute trip across town. The edges of her hairline stood up from absorbing the moisture that leaked from her scalp. Thank goodness it was 1 AM and traffic was almost nonexistent, but after not seeing Mace for two weeks she didn't want to show up at his door looking a hot mess.

Mace opened the door looking good enough for the both of them. His clear tanned skin had a bronze glow. He wore tan cargo shorts and a white tank top that clung to his torso outlining his undeniably sculpted build.

His clean cut look was something she could admire. But his swag was something she craved. So handsome and manly, he was a dream come true. Princess attempted to fix her hair, but there wasn't much she could do.

"With an outfit like that on," Mace said, "your hair is the last thing a nigga is worried about," He licked his prominent lips and she blushed. He stepped to the side and she stepped past him and entered his refreshingly cool apartment.

Princess was impressed. Just like his truck, his apartment was completely clean, too clean in her eyes. It didn't look like anyone lived there at all, more like a showroom for the building. The interior was beautifully decorated, and everything was in it's place. Beige carpets, sea green suede sofas, and modern earth toned pieces of art and vases, brought the place together like an episode on the home decorating channel. She had never been in a man's apartment that was so beautifully designed. Not knowing if she should take off her shoes or sit on the sofa, she stood in the doorway waiting for a signal from Mace.

Mace instructed her to take off her shoes and walked her over to the kitchen's bar. Even the bar stools were perfectly aligned in a row. Princess gently sat on the stool and tucked her hands onto her lap. She felt like a child scared to touch anything.

"Your place is really nice," she said, and as the words left her mouth her face flushed with embarrassment. She could tell it came off as if she had never seen nice things, and she was afraid she sounded like a hood rat.

"Thanks. I don't stay here often, just when I need too." He pulled out bottles of water for the both of them and handed her one. "You look beautiful," he said.

"I look a mess."

"A mess? Sweaty with your hair puffed up, it's exactly how I remember you. Sexy." They both laughed.

He was a smooth guy and she loved that; it made her melt. He was a nice relief from T's name calling and mistreatment. Plus Mace had a sense of humor. Facial expressions and other forms of flattering comments made her feel appreciated.

"I'm happy to see you. I thought about you the whole time I was away. You really should've been there. You have what it takes to make Miami your home."

"What do you mean I have what it takes?"

"You're sexy, adorable, you have a pretty face and a tight body. You would blend right in. Not to mention any man who saw your smile would be ready to scoop you up in an instant. I gotta get you down there."

"I would definitely go."

"Well how about Vegas?" He raised a brow.

"I would love to go to Vegas."

"Let's go then. We're going to Vegas." His enthusiasm excited her, and she hoped he was being real. He said that he traveled a lot, and if she could get a trip out of him, she would be more than willing to take it.

"Don't bullshit me," she said.

"I wouldn't do that, Princess, me and my homies are going to Vegas in a few days and I want you to come. We're bringing some girls with us and it'll be a good time. Have you ever been?"

She put her head down and stared at an imaginary spot on the carpet. "No," she said.

"Okay then, I got you. How long can you go for?"

"I don't know…I don't really have any money to go to Vegas."

"I said I got you, Princess. A beautiful girl like you needs to get used to niggas spending just to get your time, I'm good for it."

Princess was ready to leave for Vegas right then. The problem was she wasn't sure how to tell her parents that she would be going to Las Vegas with a man she barely knew. She knew they would ask a ton of questions and ultimately stop her from going. But she was out of high school now, and they needed to respect her as an adult, so one way or another she was going to find a way to go.

"Listen," Mace said, "I'm leaving in a few days, if you need a little more time to get yourself together, I'll send you a ticket. Have you ever been on a plane?"

"No."

"Well you might want to take a few shots of liquor before you get on the plane so you can go to sleep. It's a pretty long flight."

She couldn't believe he was offering her a trip. Most guys would give her a headache over a pair of shoes, and he was willing to take her on a trip? "So you're serious right now?"

"Do you want to come or not? If you're serious then I'm serious. I think Vegas would love you." Mace kissed her on the forehead and sealed the deal.

She had only seen things like this happen in movies or books that she read, but now it was really becoming a reality. How could she not agree to go on the trip?

Days passed and Princess could not to be found without Mace by her side. From dusk to dawn, the couple spent every minute riding around town, shopping, and eating at steak houses, Italian restaurants, and luxurious seafood eateries. Mace wined and dined Princess and never ceased to surprise her with spontaneous romantic gestures. He treated her like a true Princess.

She finally met her knight in shining armor. So although T would call her phone, she wasn't about to answer and ruin her fairytale story with her new Prince. Kia had called also, but Princess didn't want to hear Kia's stories. Still slightly jealous for being left behind, Princess wanted to create her own story to share and brag about before letting Kia shine on her.

Princess felt hypnotized by his trance inducing sex, and she could feel herself falling for him. Letting him get away was not an option. Anything he wanted, and any way he wanted it, Princess was at his command. After three days it was time for him to leave and go to Vegas, and time for their fairytale to end.

During most of the drive to drop Mace off at the airport, Princess remained silent. She hated the thought of separation from him but found comfort in the fact she'd join him in a couple of days. Mace reached down and caressed her bare inner thigh peeking out from beneath her sun dress. Princess, never looking away from the road, responded to his delicate gesture with a girlish smirk. She really didn't have much in Philly to look forward to now that Kia was gone, and T was no longer an option.

Mace was sweeping her off her feet, and all he asked in return was her loyalty. He reminded her that she could have anything that she wanted as long as she remained loyal to him. Her loyalty was the easiest thing she could give, and she offered it to him without reluctance.

The bag check line moved fast, so there was no time for long goodbyes. Mace's expensive luggage was piled on the sidewalk in front of them. Mace wrapped his strong arms around Princess, and she put her head on his chest with a deep sigh. He lifted her chin, looked deep into her eyes, and said, "Loyalty is everything, baby girl, and I need your commitment one hundred percent."

If loyalty was what it took to keep him then how could she refuse? "Anything for you, Mace. You have me stuck."

He must have liked her answer, because the look in his eyes softened. "Always remember," he said, "as long as you remain loyal to me, you can have anything you want." Then in an instant his look was cold steel once more. "Just don't ever give away what's mine."

An acknowledgement that she was his was more than she'd hoped for. "You know I would never do that, Mace," she said.

"Good."

He then leaned in close and pressed his soft lips to her own in a sensual kiss, gave her one last hug, then turned and strode off towards the departure gate.

Princess had a few new items, and four sexy, new bathing suits that she was ready to prance around in for everyone to see at the glitzy casino pools. Her plane ticket was for Friday, only two days away, and she was in the middle of packing her suitcase when she looked over her shoulder she saw her mother stepped in the room.

"I see you have some new bathing suits," her mother said, standing with her hands on her hips.

"Um, yea, Mom." Princess turned her back to her suitcase to avoid the disapproving expression on her mother's face, then said, "I'm going to Vegas." Her back was still facing her mother, she dreaded seeing the look on her mother's face.

"Vegas? You didn't ask me if you could go to Vegas, Princess."

"I don't have to. I'm eighteen and out of high school."

"Oh, so you're grown now?" her mother said. "Turn around; I'm talking to you."

Princess huffed and turned around. "Yes," she said, "actually, I am grown, and I'm using my own money," she lied, "so it shouldn't be a problem."

"It shouldn't be a problem?" her mother said. "Well, it is a problem. Who are you going to Vegas with and when?"

Princess let out another huff. "In four days," she said. "With Mace."

"Mace? Is that the guy that you've been running around here with?" she said. "You don't even know him."

"I do know him."

"You're not going anywhere with him."

"Yes, I am." Princess stood on her feet and faced her mother, "The ticket is already paid for. Sorry, I can't cancel it."

Her mother took a step closer to Princess. "I'd advise you to sit back down, Princess," she said with a clinched jaw. "You're barely out of school and you're making decisions like this now, huh?" Her mother's face turned a bright red. "I think you're making a mistake."

Princess sat back down and continued to place clothes in the suitcase. "I think I'm making the perfect choice."

"Well, since you think you're so grown, then maybe you should be paying bills in this house instead of spending money on trips to Vegas?"

"Okay," Princess said. "I'll put, find a job, on my to do list in Vegas."

When Friday finally arrived Princess had convinced one of her male admirers to drive her to the airport with a promise of an extra-special thank you. His round, overly-thick frame was far from Princess's taste, and she frowned as she watched the sweat caught between his body and his shirt cause the shirt to cling tightly to his bulky physique.

The fool yapped away about the big moves that he was planning to make now that he was done with high school. Princess sighed. She couldn't see him as doing anything more than remaining a taffy on some chick's stick, a straight sucker.

As promised, once they arrived at the airport and got out of the car she gave him his extra special thank you: a friendly hug. She was caught completely off guard when he wrapped her in a bear hug and smashed his dry lips against her mouth. She quickly turned her face away and leaned as far from him as his tight grip allowed.

"Damn, it's like that, Princess?"

She forced a smile in an attempt to soothe his bruised ego, and said, "I'm just not big on kissing, that's all. But thanks for the ride."

"Yeah, whatever," he said. Looking embarrassed, he retreated to his car, got in and shut the door.

Princess ignored his pouting and grabbed her bags out of the small trunk by herself. Soon enough she'd be reunited with her prince anyway. Without another glance at her rejected admirer, she strode off toward the airport entrance.

QUIANA

40

CHAPTER FOUR

Mace sat in the Venetian Hotel lobby. He tried to control his foot from tapping on the rose colored marble floor as he looked through the crowd to see if his client was coming. Twenty minutes had crept by and his client had yet to appear. Mace sighed in an effort to stay calm. Although his day was open, he hated when people wasted his time. He glanced at his watch; only a few minutes passed since the last time he had checked. He ran his hands over his white linen pants to straighten out any potential creases then scanned the room once again. With another deep sigh through a clinched jaw, he folded his arms across his white tank top and pressed his back firmly against the red lounge chair.

After a few more minutes had passed, a slender, dark-skinned man, wearing a blue button down shirt decorated with palm trees and tan dress shorts that showed off his long skinny legs, strutted into the plush hotel lobby. The straw fedora hat he wore on his head gave him the ultimate tourist appearance. The man acknowledged Mace with a giant smile and without any acknowledgement of his being a half hour late.

"Mace it's so nice to see you again," the man said in his heavy African accent. They shook hands.

"Abassi, my favorite client; how are you?" Mace said. He decided to let the issue of the late arrival go and to follow through with business.

"Today, wonderful," Abassi said. "The weather is beautiful, the women are beautiful, and I have winnings from last night. It is a good day to be me. Now, please talk quickly. I have little time to waste, money is to be made."

"I would never waste someone's time." Mace snickered.

And they say I'm arrogant. Mace gestured for Abassi to take a seat. Abassi took the seat next to Mace's and crossed his legs. Mace had met Abassi a few months before through an owner of a small café on Baltimore Avenue back in Philly.

Abassi was a businessman from Algeria whose family was involved in brewing beer. Their beer company, located in South Africa, had flourished and became one of the most popular beers in that country. The 35 year-old baby boy of three, and the only son, Abassi was the heir to the growing empire. He'd been spending a lot of time in the states hoping to make a business connect and expand their African export.

"Mace, on my last trip you showed me a phenomenal time. I am hoping to have the same experience."

He smirked at Mace with a twinkle in his eyes. Abassi was clearly hooked on Mace's product.

"Of course, Abassi, nothing but the best for you. How long are you here for?"

"I will only be here for a week, Mace. I must get back to my wife. We will be expecting soon."

"You know where to meet me," Mace said. "The price is $10,000. I'll make sure that my driver is prompt—"

"$10,000? I'm sure we can do better than that, Mace."

"Isn't that what you paid the last time?"

"Yes," Abassi said, "but I am not paying that again. I am your client, do we not have a relationship?"

"Yes, so that is the cost of our relation—"

"$4,000, that seems like a good price between friends."

Mace sneered. "Well you can have fun on the strip playing with those prices." Mace stood.

"I guess I will." Abassi rose to his feet. Mace stood face to face with Abassi calling his bluff. "Good day Mace."

"$5,000," Mace said, giving in. $5,000 was the actual price, but he told Abassi more hoping to gain something extra. "For that price," Mace said, "you will also have to provide a few cases of beer for my other clients. It's good business for you anyway."

Abassi threw his hands into the air and shrugged as if to say that's nothing. Mace ignored Abassi's arrogance and took note to start charging his new clients more, no bargaining. His clients had a weakness and a language barrier he intended to capitalize off. The two men shook hands.

"I have a friend I want you to meet," Mace said. "Her name is Kesh. She's my Dominican sex kitten. She has glowing bronze skin, no cellulite and long blonde hair. She's from Miami and definitely something you won't catch on the African shoreline." Mace knew Spanish women were rare where Abassi was from and were a fantasy realized only through porn. When Abassi nodded, Mace knew that the deal and his money were sealed for sure.

"I trust you, Mace. I know I am in good hands."

"Abassi, I am here for you. Pay the driver, and I will make sure Kesh will not let you down either. Is there anything else I can do for you?"

"Everything that I need you have already handled."

Business was going great. Mace's clients brought on new clients with every trip. Traveling to keep his contacts open had proven to be a good idea. His wealthy foreign clientele were big spenders and offered little risk. They would travel on business trips to the United States and just needed a quick fix to add spark to their drab round table meetings. Mace dialed Kesh on his cellphone knowing she was waiting for his call. Kesh loved money just as much as Mace and jumped on every opportunity to get it.

"Kesh."

"Yes, baby," She answered in her soft, Dominican accented voice.

"I need you tonight," Mace said. "There will be $1,000 waiting for you at the end of the week. Just make sure you handle him well; okay?"

"Of course, baby," Kesh said.

"His name is Abassi, he's African and has a fetish for Latin women. Speak that Spanish shit into his ear until he busts. I need him to feel like he took a journey to the Soco River."

"I promise, baby," she said, Kesh laughed. "I see you've been studying the Dominican Republic, I'm impressed. And what are we doing tonight?"

Mace quickly grabbed his penis to stop it from stiffening up. Princess would be coming into town, and in a few hours he would be reunited with his favorite toy box. Patience was a virtue that he would have to master.

"Partying like rock stars of course," Mace said. "I'll see you in the suite, everyone will be there. This will be a short night for you so don't get too wasted; I need you to be on point." Mace had zero tolerance for anyone who messed up his money. An overly drunk girl could sour a business deal. Most men were turned off by women who couldn't hold their liquor, and $5,000 was not going to be taken from Mace's plate.

"I know, Papi," she moaned. "But it does help the river flow."

"I've never heard any complaints about your river."

"Why don't you swim in it, and see for yourself?" Kesh said.

Mace licked his lips at the thought of Kesh riding his dick. "I can use another wet fountain you have." Mace said.

"Why are you torturing me? I need more than just your milk on my tongue."

"Because, you're trouble. One dip in you and you will have me and my business under water. I don't mix business with pleasure."

"But you don't have that concern with other women. I think you enjoy making me jealous."

"What I do with other women is not your problem." Mace said, clinching his fist. He hated when ho's didn't know their place.

"This is about business, Kesh."

"I'm growing impatient, Mace," Kesh whined. "I've been working for you for six months, and I want my bonus."

"You get paid well."

"I meant you," Kesh said.

"I will see you tonight, Kesh," Mace said. He ignored her wining and hung up the phone.

Princess stepped into the Las Vegas airport amazed at all of the glitz. It was nothing like Philly International. The airport had designer shops, nicer restaurants, and even slot machines inside. She followed the instructions on where to get her bags and contacted Mace to let him know she had arrived. He texted the address for where she should meet him, and she waved down a limo to take her to the hotel. Why not do it big? The limo was cheap and almost the same price as a cab. Plus it was the perfect way to kick off her first real vacation.

The ride from the Airport to the Las Vegas strip was a short one. The sun was beginning to set, but she could still see the distant mountains in the waning twilight of the clear dark evening sky. Vegas was so beautiful. There were no clouds or smog. The tall palm trees were captivating and the warm weather made her feel at home. Casino lights illuminated the Vegas strip, and people poured onto the sidewalks drinking, laughing, and having a good time. This was Vegas, baby!

Mace greeted Princess in front of the hotel looking like the king of the town. He was draped in a pair of dark denim jeans, a black Prada t-shirt, and his chest was lit up by a yellow stoned chain. Everything about him was flashy and not like his normal Philly attire. His watch, chain, and earring were all eye catchers. Even his gold framed Carrera shades blinged in the increasingly darkening sky.

Princess stepped out of the limo, in front of the Venetian hotel, wearing the Gucci glasses Mace bought her. She greeted Mace with a sultry kiss in replace of hello and anticipated the chance to give him more. He wasn't disrespectful or cheap when he tipped the limo driver or the bell hop, and he used please and thank you. She could tell Mace was familiar with staying in hotels and having others work for him. The class he demonstrated was far more than most men who were raised in the hood. He had corporate class but moved like a hustler, and that was the ultimate combo in a man.

The two stepped into the fancy hotel and made their way to Mace's suite where four men and seven stunning females awaited Princess's arrival. Princess became instantly jealous of the women in the room as soon as she saw them. Not sure if any of them were there for Mace, her instincts were to protect her interest. Mace took her around the room and introduced her to all of his friends. To her surprise, all of the women were friendly.

The women all came from different backgrounds. Some of them had clearly had some plastic surgery done, but she attributed that to the fact they were in Vegas. Flawless skin, sexy dresses, and tight hairdos, was the night's uniform. No doubt some of them were models. The men, although not all of them were attractive by her standard, were fly as well. You could tell they weren't from Philly by their style, but they were fly in their own right.

The party flowed while everyone drank on bottles of Ciroc and tooted on weed. The air in the room was thick and smoky creating a haze, but Princess felt at home. Shortly after introductions, a tall light-skin man with sandy blonde dreads made his way over to Princess with a glass of vodka and a blunt in hand. His name was CJ, and he was gorgeous: green eyes, a slim build, long locks pulled into a low pony tail, beautiful golden skin that was tanned by the Las Vegas sun, decked in lots of jewelry, and Prada from head to toe. This man gave Mace competition. He sauntered towards her and she tried not to look at him for too long, but he was too handsome to ignore.

"Wassup, Lil' mama," He said in a country accent she barely understood. He then reached his hand out for a shake. She had never seen anyone rock a grill back in Philly, but his platinum teeth dazzled with green emeralds on them. He took hold of her hand.

"Hey, how you doing?" She said, smiling and flirting with her eyes.

"Why don't you drank dis drank right here and get wit my peoples."

Her ears weren't used to hearing a down south tongue, so his words sounded like Spanish or some other foreign language. Princess looked around confused.

"I'm sorry what did you say?" She laughed "Where are you from?"

"Alabama, baby, but I live in MIA."

"Take the drink and chill with us," said a short, brown-skin girl who had introduced herself as Kitty. She had a country accent too, but it was softer on Princess's ears.

"Don't worry, Princess, sometimes I can't understand CJ either." They both laughed.

Kitty, short for Kitina, walked Princess over to one of the couches that circled the center of the suite. Her tiny legs were stacked with overly thick hips and a plump ass. Not entirely proportionate because of her small breast. Kitty was pretty, and her country accent added a sweetness to her that made her loveable within seconds of meeting her. As she briefed Princess on her familiar background with the desert, Princess admired her slanted eyes and charming smile. *Cute girl.*

"You ever been to the desert?"

"No."

"Well just watch yourself; there are wild animals lurking around and they bite." Kitty laughed at her own joke and Princess just grinned.

"On the strip?"

"No, in the desert."

Princess dismissed the girl's flat joke and turned her attention to the suite. She hadn't taken time to fully take in the room until that moment. The suite was huge. Tinted windows made up one side of the room that overlooked the Vegas strip. A round brown suede sectional couch sat in the center of the sunken living room. A crystal chandelier hung from the ceiling, and there was a kitchen, bar, and three bedrooms. The carpet was a plush tan, and abstract art work was displayed on the walls with a modern touch. The room was beautiful, like something from a scene in a music video. Mace must've been making his money in the music business because she didn't know any hustlers living like this.

Princes conversed with Kitty and the other women about shopping, make-up, and even themselves. After about an hour, only a few people remained in the suite while Princess and Mace retired to their room to prepare for the rest of the night.

The suite had two bathrooms, so there wasn't much of an issue over getting ready for the club. Mace and Princess had their own bathroom in the master bedroom, which allowed them total seclusion until they were ready to interact with everyone else.

"How do you like Vegas so far?" Mace asked. He laid on the bed with his arms wrapped around Princess's body.

Princess's mind was already made up. She didn't want to go back home. "I love it Mace," she said. "I can't believe you do this all the time."

"Well not all the time—but most of the time. Go ahead and change, you have a long night ahead, and I know that the time difference will catch up to you."

Princess forgot about the time difference. It was still early on the West coast, and back home it would almost be time for bed. She did as he suggested and took a steamy shower. She wanted Mace to join her, but instead he sat on the bed making calls. Princess tried to overhear his conversation, but the water from the shower muffled his voice.

Once out of the shower, she was crossing the room with her body and hair wrapped in towels when Mace said,

"Are you comfortable with your body?"

"Of course I am," she said. "Why'd you ask that?"

"Take your towel off then and let me watch you get dressed."

Princess let both towels fall to the carpet, and her long wavy weave dropped to the middle of her back. She wasn't embarrassed at all. T also loved watching her walk around naked, and she prided herself on her tight cheerleading body. She stood in front of him rubbing baby oil over her body, and Mace watched every move she made. Mace's lustful eyes turned her on, but she wouldn't dare make a move on him. She loved his aggression and wanted him to take control like he had that night in the car.

"Put your heels on first," he said.

Princess walked over to her suitcase and pulled out a pair of six-inch pumps covered in mirrors. She had them custom made for her trip, and they had been calling her name during the flight. Next she put on a strapless, black-laced bra and awaited Mace's approval. After receiving Mace's nod, Princess slipped on a form-fitting, one shoulder, hot-pink and white dress. The dress was another gift from Mace during their time together in Philly. He sat back with his arms folded as she fixed her hair and did her makeup.

"Sexy," Mace said. "How could anyone resist you?"

"They don't," she said. And Mace just grinned.

By the time they entered the living room, the entire party was back in the suite dressed to take over the city. Princess felt proud to be a part of the pack. They headed to the casino where the night continued.

Ching a ling ching a ling! Sounds of slot machines, dealers yelling out *winner*, and bystanders cheering on players were heard throughout the building. The men took their places around the craps table while the women stood by their sides. Everyone placed bets, some winning, some losing, but all in good spirit.

"Winner!" A rough voice yelled into the crowd as a thick mustached older man pushed chips onto the table declaring the prize winner.

After an hour of playing at the craps table, everyone's gambling bug had been satisfied, and they were all ready to leave for a nearby club. Princess and Mace, arm in arm, led their party out of the casino.

The group piled into a posh, cream Escalade stretch limo, each female seated next to a suitable man. It was obvious the crew was familiar with the driver because they all made small talk with the delightful man. Everyone appeared to be acquainted with the luxurious lifestyle except for Princess.

The driver cut through the busy traffic like a shark. *Look at me now*, a Chris Brown hit blared from inside of the club and was the perfect theme music for their arrival. Immediately, the group stepped into the VIP bottle service line, quickly made their way into the club, and over to their section which sat high above the crowd.

Princess wasn't used to this kind of upscale club. There were tons of money makers and celebrities in the VIP section. Beautiful women were everywhere. Princess almost jumped out of her dress when she saw the rapper Primo enter the VIP section with his full entourage. She kicked herself for not being able to get his attention, but she knew she was accompanying Mace, so she would have to miss out on the opportunity.

Princess swayed her hips to the sounds of hip-hop and watched Mace signal for a short Italian man to come over. The Italian man approached and shook Mace's hand. Then the two men huddled together in conversation. The Italian stood not much taller than her own 5'7" height, wore a nicely tailored charcoal-grey suit, and slicked black hair. He looked serious, like one of the mobsters on HBO. And for the past few minutes his piercing gaze had been focused on her.

She watched the Italian man nod his head to whatever Mace said. He then Mace signaled for her to come closer. When she neared, the Italian reached out for her hand. Princess placed her hand in his and was surprised when, instead of giving her a handshake like she expected, he kissed her hand like a gentleman in the old movies.

"And your name is?" he asked.

"Princess."

"Very nice, Princess. You look a bit young to be in this club. How old are you?"

Not sure if she should disclose her real age, she looked to Mace. He nudged her to continue the conversation, so she answered, "18."

"18, very nice. You are a beautiful girl, Princess. I am friends with Mace, my name is Antonio." Although the club was loud, she could still pick up on his Italian accent over the booming speakers.

Mace watched their interaction. Not sure if Antonio was some kind of test, she kept the conversation brief.

"Champagne for a Princess," Antonio said. He waved one of the cocktail waitresses over and took a glass from her tray.

"Oh, no." Princess shook her head, "I have had enough, really."

"You don't drink?" He asked.

"Yes, I drink."

"Then why you say no?"

"Take the drink Princess," Mace said with authority. Princess took the glass and sipped the sweet pink champagne.

"You don't have to be afraid of me, Princess," Antonio said. "We're all family here." He then turned and walked off.

Princess finished the champagne then followed it up with three more glasses. Before she knew it, her wobbly legs could barely hold her up. Princess became more social with every glass, and found herself mixed in with the crowd. She partied with the girls and made new friends. She kept her distance from the men, but she could still feel their eyes on her.

"Let's head out," Mace said into Princess's ear. "We have business to tend to."

Mace grabbed hold of Princess's hand and escorted her towards the club's exit before she could ask any questions. Drunk with booze, she didn't care about any of the other girls. She just wanted her time alone with Mace so she could show her appreciation for a wonderful trip.

"You wanna take a ride in the limo?" Mace asked. "You should get a better view of Nevada."

"Sounds wonderful, Mace."

The idea of just the two of them chasing the city lights together in a decked out limo was as romantic as it could get in her eyes. Mace was giving her a night that she would never forget.

The limo was no longer moving when Princess woke up. She dozed off during their ride around the city, and now she was unsure about how long she had been asleep. She sat up to see if they had arrived at the hotel and rubbed her eyes to adjust to the view outside of the window. What she saw was a dry desert and a lonely two-lane highway. Princess's head was pounding from the after effects of the alcohol, and her dry mouth yearned for salivation. Mace sat unalarmed and emotionless, looking at her.

"Where are we?" Princess asked.

"I wanted to show you where I usually stay when I come to Vegas," Mace said.

Princess scanned the desert through the dark limo tint but there wasn't a house in sight. There was nothing but mountains and highway for miles, and the only car on the road aside from their limo was the one creeping in their direction from a distance. It was late and the highway was almost pitched black.

"Why did we stop?" she asked.

Knots turned in Princess's stomach from the coldness of Mace's distant demeanor. Princess was being timid. This part of the trip was unexpected; and for the first time, she felt vulnerable, in Mace's presence. Mace reached into a compartment under the wine bar and pulled out a piece of black fabric. He ran his fingers over the cloth then straightened the material until it stretched length wise across his hands.

"Because you have to put on a blindfold." he said, as if it was a perfectly normal answer.

"A blindfold for what?"

"I can't have you seeing where I live."

"Why the hell not?"

"Because, I don't know who you could bring there in the future. If you plan on being around, you will learn where it is, but I have to make sure I can trust you."

"What is it that you're not telling me about yourself, Mace?"

"I've told you everything that you need to know for now. This isn't a debate, Princess, put on the blindfold." He tossed it to her but she didn't budge. Her eyes were fixed on him while the dark cloth lay in her lap.

"Princess, either you put the blindfold on or get left on the highway. You can't see where my house is yet."

Princess still didn't move. Sweat sprouted from her palms as she remained focused on Mace and tried to keep her composure. The situation was too weird, and she was owed more of an explanation. Maybe he was some famous person that she wasn't aware of; or maybe he was gang associated, and that's how he knew the little Italian man? Whoever he was, he wasn't taking her anywhere with a blindfold on.

She looked straight into his eyes and said, "No."

"Then get out," Mace said.

She looked around for her bag; her phone was still inside of it. But the bag was gone. "Where's my stuff?"

"I have it and you will get it back at the house. Put the blindfold on."

"No, give me my bag." Princess tried to mind her tone but she was frustrated. Back home she heard tales of girls being abducted. Only, she would never make the 6 o'clock news back in Philly if this was the case.

"Why are you being so difficult?" Mace asked.

"Didn't you promise me loyalty? Didn't I take you shopping and show you a good time? You came all the way to Vegas to see me, and now you don't trust me? Princess, you have nothing in your bag that I need. Put the blindfold on and you will get your stuff at the house. We could've been on our way there if you'd just do as daddy said."

Princess refused to give in. She was scared. He wasn't acting like the warm fun Mace that she had gotten to know. His icy words no longer complimented his sparkling eyes. He was ordering her around and talking with direct authority. Princess sat for another minute. She glanced over at Mace, who was rapidly tapping his foot, and she could tell his patience was growing thin.

He reached in his pants and pulled out a black handgun. Princess froze. Her heart beat sped up and tears filled her eyes. She couldn't get a grip on herself. She shook her head at the scene playing out before her eyes. She bit down on her lip and tried not to cry, but the tears came anyway.

"I'm not going to hurt you, Princess, but I do have to protect my interest. I need you to follow my directions; okay?" Mace took the safety off the gun and put it in his lap. Princess covered her mouth with one hand and nodded in silence as tears fell onto her fingertips. "It is important that you listen to me," Mace said, "and trust that I am capable of doing anything you can think of." She nodded again, not wanting to set him off. "Okay, good. Put the blindfold on."

Trembling in fear, Princess followed his instructions and put the blindfold on. He took her hands and tied them together with another piece of cloth, and tugged her blindfold to make sure that it was secure. More tears dampened the blindfold as they drove off in silence.

Mace talked to her during the entire drive in a cool calm manner as if everything was normal. He discussed the night they just had, future places he wanted to go, and even made a few jokes. He attempted to make her as comfortable as possible.

Princess couldn't relax. She was riding down a two-lane desert highway. She had thought Mace was her prince, and instead of listening to her mother had found out the hard way she had no idea who Mace really was. Mace could talk about protecting his estate all he wanted, she felt as though she was being kidnapped.

"Dear Lord, I ask that you save my soul," she whispered, "As you welcome me into your gates, I pray that my walk in your light was that of a good servant. I know that I have made mistakes, but I pray for your forgiveness. Amen."

It was a short ride before the limo arrived at their destination. Mace escorted Princess out of the elevated limo, catching her as she tripped from the high ledge. She couldn't see anything. Her only guide was the gentle prodding of Mace's hand on the middle of her back. Princess wasn't sure what to expect. The sun beamed on her shoulders, telling her it was early morning. The dry air had a fresh clean scent, but there was nothing that distinctly stood out and gave her hints to her surroundings. Suddenly, Mace put a hand on her shoulder, stopping her. She heard the jingle of keys, the tumble of a lock, and then a door being opened. Next, she felt a draft of cool air and a quick nudge from Mace who prompted her to keep moving. The distinct clacking sound of her heels against hardwood floors informed her they were inside a house. And the echoes of their footsteps made the house sound large end empty.

"Almost there, Princess," Mace said, "just take it one step at a time."

One step at a time, Princess carefully made her way up the stairwell. With tied hands she held tight to the metal banister. The two finally made it to the top of the steps and entered a room. Mace eased Princess onto a bed, untied her hands, and finally removed her blindfold.

"See, Princess, no harm." His words weren't the least bit comforting to her ears.

She looked around the room. A dresser, mirror, and end tables passed the room off as an ordinary bedroom. The sheets and comforter that made up the bed were a pattern composed of black and tan blocks and sat upon cherry wood furniture, which was the universal wood throughout the room. Through the doorway off to one side of the room she saw a bathroom. There were speakers that hung from the ceiling, but she didn't see a TV. Out of all the things in the room, what stood out the most was a brown and black zebra lounge chair that sat in the corner.

"Mace, please tell me what's going on? Whose room is this?"

"Whose room do you think this is?" Mace said. "It's yours."

Princess, clueless to what he could've meant, gathered her thoughts on how to approach him without pissing him off. He had already proved he had a short temper, and was quick to pull out a gun, two things she wanted to avoid.

"Mace, I'm confused. Is this your house?"

"Yea, this is mine; this is your house too." His face never changed; his blank eyes gave no clue to what thoughts were forming in his mind. He wasn't smiling or trying to charm her anymore. Everything that came out of his deceitful mouth was stated as fact.

"How can this be my room?" Princess said.

"All the girls have a room," Mace said.

"What girls?"

"Yani, Kitty, Kesh; do I need to name all of them?"

The images of the girls ran through Princess's mind like mug shots flashing on a screen. "Why do they stay here? Where are they now?"

"Princess, you said you needed a job, didn't you?"

She could see from the look on his face he was becoming frustrated with her. He glared at her as if daring her to deny what he'd said; he stood there waiting for her to answer.

"Yes, Mace, I said it. But what kind of job? What's going on?"

"Get some rest, Princess. You have to work this evening."

"What are you talking about, Mace?"

Her fear turned to tears once again. She was far away from home, no phone, no one knew where she was, she didn't know anyone she was with, and the person she'd trusted was the cause of the whole predicament. She was clueless about what hole her life was being tossed into, and her head ached from just thinking about it all.

"You don't want to work?" Mace asked.

"Doing what?"

"Calm down, Princess. There's no need to cry. You're getting yourself worked up for nothing. All you have to do is assist me with my clients. It's not that hard; don't worry."

"Don't worry? What do you mean by assisting?"

His expression hardened. "Don't act naïve, Princess. It's simple; you're going to fuck, and suck, and do whatever the clients want."

"What?"

"Yani will be here later to educate you on everything."

She couldn't believe what she was hearing. The problem was her vulnerability. She had no transportation or plane ticket, and no one knew where she was; he had it all planned out.

"Mace, I ain't no ho."

"Princess, don't act like you never fucked nobody. I pay my girls good, more money than you could get at some fucking clothes store."

"I can't believe this. All the wining and dining was just a scheme to get me to your whore house? You kidnapped me to turn tricks for you?"

"So now you're above trickin? Since when? Since you got a trip after fucking a nigga? Or did you get above it when you let me hit on the first night? I'm confused Princess, what makes you any better than any tramp on the streets? At least I'm talking 'bout some real money. Not that sneaker and shoe shit you're used to. Ain't nothing in this world free, baby; I hate to break it to you. You thought you were gonna get an easy come up just like the rest? Everybody has to work." He turned his back on her with those harsh words, left the room, and slammed the door behind him.

Princess sat on the bed trying to piece the puzzle together. He was right. She had been moving like a prostitute. Why wouldn't think he would be down? But at this point, did what Mace thought even matter? Hell no. What she needed to do was think of a way to get out of this mess.

The turn of the door handle interrupted Princess's deep sleep. Through slighted eyes, she watched the door from where she lay on the bed, waiting to see who her intruder was. If need be, she was ready to attack. The intruder turned out to be the tall, dark- skinned, curvaceous beauty called, Yani. She watched Yani quietly close the door back and then sashay over towards her. Before eye contact could be made, Princess shut her eyes and pretended to be asleep. She felt Yani lean over her, then heard Yani walk away and fumble around opening and closing the dresser drawers. The woman was wearing heels so every move she made could be tracked.

"Princess, wake up," Yani said, poking Princess in the arm. Princess rolled over and locked eyes with the smiling woman.

Yani's smile was fake, and Princess had no intentions on participating in her game. They weren't friends. They didn't even know each other, and this damn sure wasn't the time to start making new acquaintances. Princess scowled at Yani. Yani shrugged and moved away from the bed.

The woman was indeed one of the working jewels in Mace's jewelry box. Her skin was flawless, smooth and dark; and she had wide hips and large breast. Her waist was tiny and her stomach flat, as if she ate nothing but lettuce. Long lean legs made up the majority of her body and her full lips were covered in clear lip gloss. She wasn't wearing as much makeup as she had worn the night before. The long black weave she wore with the bang going across her forehead gave her a stylish appearance. No doubt she was just a regular pretty girl underneath all of the mascara and foundation. The duck that you grew up with but you never noticed her swan qualities until puberty, when her body made the perfect complement to her changing face. Her smile was innocent although Princess knew her intentions weren't. Yani took a seat on the tan and black chair.

"Don't sit in that chair," Princess said.

Yani stood. "Then can I sit on the bed?"

Princess watched Yani and remained cautious.

"Well," Yani said, "Mace sent me here to give you a crash course on house rules. It's really simple."

Princess turned her back to Yani.

"Listen," Yani said, "it's either you open your ears, or you're going to be in for a rude awakening."

Princess didn't care about any rude awakening Yani could've been talking about. She was already experiencing a rude awakening.

"First off," Yani said, "there's seven girls in the house including me. It's me, Kesh, Kitty, Candy, Lala, Gigi, and Hanna; and you make eight. We're like a family here, Princess, we don't step on each other's toes. Every girl has her own room. There's three bedrooms in the basement, three on the first floor, and five on the second floor. You probably didn't notice there's no dining room, it existed until Hanna came, and they turned it into her room." She laughed to herself. "Mace, Ro, and CJ stay on the second floor with us. You met Ro and CJ at the party, and of course you already know Mace."

"There's only one thing I need to know from you, Yani," Princess said.

"What's that?" Yani asked, perking up now that Princess finally responded.

"How do I get out of here?"

For a moment the only sound Princess heard in response was the other woman's breathing. "Well," Yani said, "Mace told me to tell you he isn't holding you against your will."

Princess turned around to catch Yani's expression and was surprised to see the sincere look on the woman's face. It gave Princess hope, and she sat up in the bed. "Then I'm ready to leave now."

The sad smile that crossed Yani's face told Princess that she must have somehow misunderstood. "Princess, I'm sorry. It's not that simple."

"You said I could leave, right?"

"Yes, but let me explain everything so you can understand."

Princess nodded.

"Good," Yani said. "We get clients, usually the same ones until they leave town. These men are paid, Princess, and we get paid very well for our services. Most are foreigners or frequently travelling businessmen. They want a companion during their time in Vegas. They request a girl and stick with her until they leave. Treat the client right, and every trip they make to Vegas you will be compensated a little more, and even offered gifts. Let them talk to you as if you're their girlfriend. Have fun, joke and laugh, make sure they feel comfortable. The moment they feel like a trick you will no longer be a treat."

"Hold on, Yani," Princess said. "Why are you telling me about clients? I only need to know about leaving."

"And I promise, I'll get to that, but first let me tell you about—"

"No, Yani. First, tell me how I can get the hell out of here."

Yani sighed. "Okay," she said. "Mace said that once you pay back the money for your trip, you can go home. To do that, he said, you need a week's worth of work. You already have your first client scheduled for six o'clock for two hours, and you will have him until Wednesday. That's how much time the client bought, but he will be in town until Friday. So, if you really want to get the hell away from here like you said, charm this guy and get him to pay for the two other days he'll be in town, and you'll be on your way back home."

Yani looked at Princess as if waiting for a response. But what was there to say? Mace had planned everything perfectly. Even if she just wanted to leave, he'd still get what he wanted; she'd still end up his ho.

QUIANA

CHAPTER SEVEN

Beep, beep, beep. The alarm clock went off and Princess slowly counted to three before she opened her eyes. She still hoped for a magical fairy to appear and let her know it had all been a bad dream. But instead the room was dim, no flying mini people in sight. It was 4 PM and she had slept most of the day away. She slipped out of the covers and into a pair of soft pink slippers that were placed at the foot of the bed. Then she walked over to the mirror, and looked at her reflection. Her eyes were puffy from all the crying. If what Yani said was real, and what Yani said was true, she didn't look the least bit presentable to be in a man's presence.

"Mirror, mirror, how the hell did I get here?"

She rubbed her hands over her face and sighed. Before Princess had let Yani out of the room, she made sure the other woman gave her the run-down on everything she needed to do. And Princess had paid close attention too. If what she had to do to get back home and be safe was have sex with someone, then that's what she'd do. Princess tiptoed over to the bedroom door and opened it just enough to stick her head out. Sweet aromas of chicken baking in the oven tempted her nostrils. She could hear sounds of laughter coming from downstairs.

Princess closed the door and walked over to the dresser to see what was inside. Just like Yani told her, the drawers were stocked with a few pairs of jeans, white and black tank tops, and lots of panties and lingerie. Someone, her guess was Mace, had taken the time to place all of the shoes she had packed for her Las Vegas trip in the closet but her bags weren't there. Apparently, Mace worked out every detail way before the limo ride. Time was flying by and it was going on 5 o'clock. Princess remembered that the guy she had to have sex with to get home would be arriving at six, so she needed to start getting ready.

After she showered, put on a touch of makeup, a spray of Burberry perfume, and dressed herself in a pair of jeans and a white tank top like Yani had instructed, she sat down on the bed to wait.

It wasn't long before she heard a tap at the door, and Yani walked in. Yani carried a tray of baked chicken, string beans and brown rice; and a plate of steak, string beans and potatoes. Yani looked surprised to see Princess was dressed.

"Dinner is here," Yani sang, placing the food and a bottle of gin that was tucked under her arm on the dresser. Princess couldn't hold back her smile. Princess wanted to rip through the meal and crack open that bottle ASAP.

"We only eat healthy around here, so the steak is for your client; okay? No eating until he gets here which should be in about five minutes. I just came to drop everything off. You look great Princess, don't be nervous, you'll do fine." She hurried out the room before Princess could respond.

A few minutes later the door knob turned and a well-dressed man came into the bedroom. It was Antonio.

Princess remembered the Italian man from the club the night before. Seeing his sneaky grin made her angry. Now their meeting last night made sense. He was scoping her out at the club with Mace's help.

"Hey baby," he said, "remember me?"

She paused for a second before answering; as much as she wanted to curse him out, he was her ticket home. She knew she had to charm him at any cost.

"Yes, I remember you," she said. "Antonio, right?"

The man nodded.

"I'll just call you Tony." She smiled, trying her best to disguise her anger.

"No," he said, frowning. "You will call me Antonio."

"Okay, Antonio. How are you today?"

"Is that my food?" He walked over to the dresser and lifted his plate. Without hesitation he sat on the bed and dug into the food as if it was his last meal. "Pour me some gin."

Princess looked at him like he was crazy then checked her attitude. He had the money. She sashayed past him, picked up the bottle of gin from the dresser, and poured him a glass.

"Do you mind if I eat?" she asked, handing him the glass of strong liquor.

"No, not right now, baby," he said without looking up from his food. She was starving and wanted the eat bad, but she had been warned by Yani to follow his rules. She poured herself a tall glass of the clear liquor, knowing that he wouldn't object.

She wanted to make both of them more comfortable, so she asked, "You want a massage?"

"I don't have that much time, baby. Put on some black shoes and panties. No bra."

She marked his request as another test of Mace's. Mace knew what Antonio would like, that was why he asked her to walk the room nude last night in the suite. Antonio turned on the radio and found a hip hop station.

Princess laughed. "You like this music?"

"Yes; you don't like it?"

"Of course, but I didn't think you would."

"Baby, I like lots of black things," Antonio said, then grabbed the bulge in the front of his pants.

Princess rolled her eyes and laughed. In some strange way she found that gesture flattering. She made her way to the bathroom and returned dressed as he requested, black thong panties and black shoes, no bra.

His eyes zeroed in on her round breast and hard nipples. She bounced across the room, waiting for his next request. He didn't say anything; he just watched her prance around.

It felt good to have his attention and to see his response to her body. Princess had never been with a white man, or anyone who wasn't black. Never before had she considered that her curvy body would be lusted after by a foreigner. She could see his cock growing in his tight pants, and his arousal was arousing her also, but not enough to get her wet. She grabbed the gin. Then with her back turned to Antonio, she squatted in front of him with her knees spread wide. Princess flung her hair behind her and drunk the gin straight from the bottle.

"Easy, baby," Antonio said.

His words let her know she was turning him on. He grabbed her soft bottom and squeezed it. Snatching the bottle out of her hand, he took a swig of the liquor, then sat the bottle down and ran his hands over her shoulder and down to her breast. She found herself getting turned on. She placed the back of her head on his knee to allow him to get a better feel of her melons.

Princess stood up, then bent over and bounced her ass like a dancer in a music video. He rubbed her ass while she made it clap to the rythem of the music.

"Get up here on the bed with me," he said.

Princess quickly hopped on the bed. Antonio didn't hesitate. He slid his pants to his ankles, pulled out his penis and put on a condom with urgency. To her surprise he wasn't as small as she had suspected. He was perfectly built, not too small, not too thick, and when he inserted her, she instantly knew she would enjoy the sex.

He was easy to please, and since she needed the stress reliever anyway, she began to look forward to working with him. Antonio went wild every time they had sex that week. Back shots and eating her pussy was all that he wanted to do in their time together. He would compliment her on her smooth brown skin while falling in love with her juicy fruit. She realized that she was having just as much fun as he was, plus he would leave her a $100 tip every time. As she had hoped, he requested her for additional days, and before she knew it she had paid off her debt.

After a week with Antonio, Mace stepped into the room grinning from ear to ear. They hadn't spoken much since the day he pulled the gun on her. Princess went out of her way to keep her distance.

A lot of anger towards Mace brewed inside of her. Still, somehow his charming ways and good looks softened up her feelings towards him. As Mace strutted into the room, Princess fixed her eyes on him. She remained guarded. Mace was as predictable as a hungry pit bull. His hard boots hit the hardwood floors as he strode towards her.

"I hate to see you go, Princess. Tell me you'll stay?" Mace touched her cheek with the affectionate touch of a lover.

"Mace, I'm ready to go home."

Mace shrugged his shoulders and nodded his head. "I said I wouldn't hold you against your will, and I'm a man of my word."

Princess, pleased with his response almost jumped into his arms, but then she remembered what he was agreeing to. Going home shouldn't have been a privilege or something that she should've been kept away from. She should've never been forced into the house, and should've never went to Vegas with him in the first place.

"Be ready by 6 a.m.," he said. "The driver will be outside waiting for you. Your bags will already be in the car."

Princess nodded her head. It bothered her that she felt grateful to him. The same spark that had twinkled in his eyes like stars over a still lake had returned, and though it made no sense, she also felt her old feelings towards Mace returning too. Princess closed her eyes and tried to fight her feelings.

"Princess," he said, "I really don't want you to go."

Mace then embraced Princess and kissed her on the lips. He was being forceful yet erotic, and the urge to succumb to his power was growing harder to fight. She couldn't help but reflect on the times they had sex back in Philly. She tried to resist her cravings for him, but Mace cuffed her vagina with his thick palm until her wetness soaked through her panties.

"I need you, Princess," Mace said. "I need you to be my queen."

His words tickled her ear lobe as a tug of war between her mind and body ensued. Mace's words were sensual, and his movements were entrancing, and once again she found herself falling for him. She tried to push him back, but his grip on her arms only grew firmer. Princess attempted to wiggle away from Mace but she wasn't mentally or physically strong enough. She wanted Mace more than ever despite who he really was. Something about his bad ways was sexy, appealing, and what she wanted in her life.

"Stop fighting it, Princess. This is your castle and I am your king."

He forced her body down onto the bed and pinned her arms above her head. Princess stopped fighting. Inside she still saw Mace as the handsome charismatic man she met in the bar. She was still angry with him, but her body needed him. She needed to see him the way she saw him before. She wanted to hold on to the person she believed he was. Mace lifted her mini black nightgown from her body and pulled her drenched panties down. Princess was naked and at his will. Mace wasted no time. He took his clothes off and climbed on top of her inviting body.

As soon as she saw his naked body she clinched her vagina in anticipation of his bronze thick penis. Her anger towards Mace poured out of her body as their bodies melted together. It was makeup sex. The harder she thrust her pussy at him, the harder he stroked, keeping her under his control. He held on tight as he dug deep, and left her to do nothing but yell out confused by pleasure and pain.

Mace gazed into her eyes when he molded his hands around her neck and squeezed until she was just short of choking. He told her over and over that he needed her by his side. He was extremely rough, and his gentle words did not match his forceful actions, but Princess enjoyed the pain. She wanted to believe him. He fucked her harder and more powerfully with every stroke.

"I can't let you go, Princess," he moaned. "I need you."

Sex with Mace was such a powerful whirlwind there was no way she could escape. The sparks, suggestive voice, and irresistible sex caused her to reply to every question thrown her way exactly the way he wanted. Mace was fucking her like he loved her, and deep down inside of her she wanted that to be true. He quickly pulled out and forced his penis into her mouth until he exploded all over her tongue. They repeated the sex over and over again for the rest of the night until Princess was convinced of his need for her, and then against what she knew to be her better judgment she agreed to stay.

QUIANA

80

CHAPTER EIGHT

"What are you doing?" Yani whispered harshly into Kesh's ear.

Kesh half turned and put a finger to her lips, signaling Yani for keep quiet. She then put her ear back to the door.

Curious about what Kesh was hearing, Yani pressed her ear against the door too. Turned off by what she heard, Yani yanked Kesh's arm and pulled her away from the door. She had no interest in getting caught listening to someone having sex in the house.

"Yani, get off of my arm," Kesh whispered, snatching her arm away from Yani.

"What is wrong with you?" Yani whispered back.

"Nothing is wrong with me."

Kesh turned and ran down the steps, to her bedroom and Yani followed behind her as quietly as possible not wanting to interrupt Mace and set him off.

Yani stepped into Kesh's bedroom right behind Kesh and closed the door. Kesh sat on the bed and folded her arms across her chest. Kesh was new and a lot different than the other girls. For everyone else in the house, what they did was simply a job; but for Kesh it was a lifestyle. She never took a day off and needed to be known as the highest paid and the best fuck in the house. Expensive bags, designer labels, full makeup day in and day out, you would've thought she lived on a photo shoot. She went about her business like she would be getting an Oscar for the best performance.

"Kesh, why were you listening at Princess's door?"

"Princess is in my place, Yani."

Kesh was clearly delusional. Everyone knew she was infatuated with Mace, but listening to him have sex was beyond mere infatuation. Yani felt bad for the naïve woman.

"Kesh, it's Mace were talking about."

"So?"

"So that's our boss, nothing else. So what if he fucks Princess? She'll be fucking one of his clients tomorrow. It's just business. I know his game; that's how he controls the girls, especially when they're new." Yani recalled the girls that had come and gone under Mace's regime. Because CJ was her cousin, she never had to succumb to any of the boss's sexual needs.

"Mace is scared to fuck me," Kesh said.

Yani frowned. She had never heard such a thing. Yani took a seat next to Kesh and waited to hear more of Kesh's fairytale.

"I know you don't believe me," Kesh said, "but he is. When I fuck him, I'm gonna take all that money he has. Shopping sprees and trips for me and my boo. I might even get him to leave this game alone. Nah, fuck that. He can stay in the game, as long as mama getting some of that cake. You girls can work under my reign."

"I can see you put a lot of thought into this," Yani said. She laughed at Kesh's imagination.

"Hell yeah. I have so much fun when I'm out with Mace. He's never had to check me like the rest of you bitches; I play my part. That's why he keeps me close. He told me, if he fucks me, he's gonna get caught up, and then—" She clapped her hands together loudly. "It's curtains."

"Kesh, Mace will never be your man. He'll never be Princess's or any woman's man. He's a pimp, Kesh. I don't know what that means in your native tongue, but to us Yankees it means a man that you don't think about settling down with. On top of that, you're a ho If anybody marries you it's gonna be somebody who is far from your present and knows nothing about your past."

"Do you ever think about how much money they make a week?" Kesh asked. "There are eight girls in the house; each client pays at least $5,000 for a week, depending on the girl and what he wants. Me, I'm one of the most expensive pieces of ass this house ever owned. I already know Mace charges at least $6,000 just to touch this Latina heat." Kesh snapped her fingers in front of Yani's face with pride.

"Yea, we all know they get money," Yani said.

"Get money isn't the word. They are milking these foreigners for major paper. I need more than $1,000 a week. Every king needs a queen and I am the perfect fit." Kesh smiled. "If you're lucky, I might let you stick around and upgrade your price."

Yani was getting tired of the crazy talk. Why a woman would want to train a dog was beyond her understanding. Besides, she always thought Kesh would be more of a cat person.

"Listen, Kesh, whatever it is that you want with Mace, go for it, but don't mess up what you have going for yourself. Princess is in his eye right now. She's new and a few years younger than you, which means fresh. Just get whatever money you can while you can. They only keep girls here until they're 25. So if I was you I would stack and make a plan. I've seen too many girls leave with nothing and go back to turning tricks for some small time pimp, boyfriend, or strip club. Designer bags and jewels ain't nothing when you don't have a real roof. You're what, 24 now? Mace is giving you one good year to make your shit pop, probably because you are undeniably a dime. But don't be dumb. Setting your sights on taking over his hard work is a long shot, and last I checked, you don't even own a gun."

"You're about to turn 25 too, right?" Kesh asked. "So what do you plan on doing?"

Yani curled up her lip unsure on how to answer the question. She knew that her time in the house was coming up, and she pushed the thought to the back of her mind. As much as she hated having sex with strangers, she hated the thought of working a regular job and paying bills even more. She had become dependent on the lifestyle. Stepping back into the real world would be like a baby being thrown into the ocean.

Yani reflected on how she ended up at the house. It was just after she dropped out of college. With no parents, and no siblings, CJ took her in, not wanting to leave his little cousin in Alabama alone. Plus, he figured his smart and beautiful little cousin Yani, who was 21 at the time, would make the perfect secretary. He and his partners needed someone they could trust, and Yani was an orphan with no real reason to stay in Alabama, and she needed some money.

CJ was only a few months older but way more street savvy. He tried to put Yani onto the game but she wanted to become one of the girls instead of a secretary. She saw more opportunity to make more money by turning tricks. CJ's partners Mace and Ro explained to her that if she wanted to be down, there was no backing out. Without CJ's knowledge, she began taking on clients left and right, trying to get her cake up. By the time CJ realized that his partners were sneaking around giving her clients behind his back, she was already in the game. He was hurt that his little cousin would go that route, but *ho's gonna be ho's,* and in her eyes every woman was a dick and a few dollars away from being just that.

"I guess I'll start a business," Yani said.

"A business?" Kesh asked, frowning. "What kind of business?"

"I don't know. A nail salon, maybe a shoe store. I was in school ya know? And I still keep the books for the house. I even know how much you make." She rolled her eyes at Kesh's doubtful look. "I've been stacking for the past two years, so whatever I do, I'm gonna be all right."

"My time will never be up sweetie," Kesh said. "I'm the heiress to the throne."

Yani was done with the foolishness and saw her efforts to school Kesh as pointless. Kesh wanted her fairytale, so who was she to tell her any different.

"Well," Yani said, "the king ain't worried about his queen right now. He's focused on a Princess."

CHAPTER

NINE

"What's up, brah?" CJ asked Mace, as they sat at the table watching the Latin dancers twirl to the sounds of reggae-tone. The mix of Hip Hop and Latin music was hard on Mace's popping ears. He tried to ignore the Spanish rap as it flooded his ear ways, but the foreign sounds only rattled his bones the more he thought about not listening to it. Mace sat and watched the crowd. He wasn't paying CJ any mind; he purposefully hesitated to answer CJ, knowing there was much more behind the question.

"Chillen," Mace said, blowing off the question and focusing deeper on a wide hipped Mexicana with dark features. She wore nothing but a belly shirt and black spandex shorts that showed the crease of her ass in the shine of the club's light as she rocked her body against her dance partner. Her basketball ass was surely bought along with the perfect set of double D's planted on her chest. As the woman rocked her body against her dance partner, she locked eyes with Mace. Flinging her hair back and forth, she fixed her lips and blew Mace a kiss.

Mace knew a stripper when he saw one, and he was considering putting her on the team. He was also considering something more important: putting Princess on the bench for a while.

He knew he had gone too far with Princess, and had grown too attached. No way she was going home. But maybe after Yani left, Princess could take her spot.

Over the past month, the thought of other men huffing and grunting while tearing her box apart had become harder for Mace to accept. Mace's jealousy was growing stronger by the day, and jealousy was not an emotion to fool around with. For the first time in years he wanted a woman to himself. Yea, he knew it would be breaking the rules, but when you're a boss you make your own rules. Sleeping with Princess and buying her gifts was becoming something he looked forward to doing. He didn't know how it happened, but cupid was playing a trick on him for sure. Popped him right in the ass and kept it moving. Love is blind, but Mace had two eyes, so he knew not to be dumb. Giving up control over a woman was never an option, first opportunity she got she would fly like a caged bird and sing to everyone she knew. Jail was not an option either. Two things he would never let a chick make him lose, money or freedom.

"I said what's up, brah?" CJ said again, interrupting Mace's thoughts with his commanding tone.

Mace looked over at the young nigga with so much heart. Mace was only 5 years his senior but looked at CJ like a baby boy. CJ had big balls stepping to him that way. He was like a little step brother, yea, they were close, but not blood. CJ had been getting out of line lately, testing his patience, and questioning his decisions. Mace knew CJ was looking at him like he was weak because of the way he was handling Princess, but it was his house and she was his bitch, in his eyes anyway.

"We got a problem or something?" Mace asked.

"Nah, we ain't got no problem, brah. I'm just asking what's up? I didn't know we was taking bitches personal because if so, there's something in the house I need to put on my lap." CJ grabbed his crotch.

Mace scratched his head in efforts to control his hands. If he hit CJ, it really would be something personal, but he wasn't going to be disrespected either. He slid his hands down his face, to his chin, and took a deep breath.

"The walls is the only thing that should be minding what's going on in my room," Mace said.

"Well maybe those walls should get a lil thicker 'cause I was jacking off all night listening to Princess." CJ laughed as he imitated moaning sounds and humped the air.

"Nah, that was Yani," Mace said, knowing CJ always suspected that Mace had fucked his cousin.

CJ clinched his jaw and the game was over.

Mace lightly backhanded CJ on his chest. "Oh, we takin bitches personal now?"

CJ stood up from the table with his fist balled, chest heaving and nostrils flared. He ran his fingers over his dreadlocks and locked eyes with Mace.

"You gonna fight over a bitch?" Mace shouted, cracking his knuckles. "I thought we had jokes? Go take a walk, CJ."

CJ turned away and started to walk off; then suddenly, he stopped. Mace looked in the direction CJ was facing, and he immediately understood the reason for CJ's pause when he saw a slick haired Spanish man cha cha'ing their direction. The husky man was immaculate in his tight black dress pants and peach button down shirt. The man continued to dance and sing to the music as he got closer to the table. CJ looked back at Mace with his face screwed up more than a Rubik's cube.

"Matter of fact stay here," Mace said to CJ. Mace stood to his feet as the man greeted him with a hug.

"Mace!" The man cried. "CJ!"

When the man tried to hug CJ, CJ stepped back and stuck his hand out for a handshake. Mace looked at CJ. CJ usually followed the flow of the customers, not wanting to disrespect them. It could mean the difference in a deal or no deal.

"CJ we're not friends no more? Give me a hug!" The big, jolly Ricky Martin transitioned CJ's handshake into a hug. CJ shook his head at Mace, and Mace watched with a grin. "Sit," the man said. "Please."

The man waved his long arm, beaming with a gaudy gold Rolex, towards the table. He snapped his fingers and a petite waitress rushed to his side.

"Yes, Javier?" She asked, pulling out her pen.

"Bring me a cold bottle of Jose Cuervo," Javier said to the waitress. Then to Mace and CJ, "Are you gentlemen hungry?"

They shook their heads no.

"Tequila and lime shrimp for me, mami," Javier said, adding a swift smack to the waitress's ass.

"Mace, CJ, tell me what's new? I'm only here for a few days and I need one of your beautiful girls to show me a good time."

Mace couldn't understand why a man so connected and always surrounded by beautiful women needed to pay five grand to have a treat for a few days. He wasn't like the typical clients they received. Javier had lots of Mexican American friends and family in the states, and he was a very frequent visitor. The women in the club would've loved to be affiliated with any of the *Loco Dias Brothers* from Mexico. They had the west coast flooded with their red bud marijuana, and Tijuana was their kingdom. With family ties to politics, the brothers were a deadly force to be reckoned with and virtually untouchable. But Javier was spending more and more time in the states and Mace wanted to know why.

The waitress scurried over to the table almost spilling the opened bottle. She quickly gathered herself together as she acknowledged both CJ and Mace with a wink. They were gaining a reputation with the girls for being big tippers as well. No drink was served without a wink and licking of the lips to gain their attention. CJ placed a $20 bill in her shorts and gently squeezed her ass.

"Gracias, papi," the waitress said.

"Gotta love the ho's," CJ said.

"What can we do for you Javier?" Mace said. He swallowed a shot of the Tequila and motioned the waitress to pour another shot before waving her to leave.

"I need something new," Javier said. "I need something fun. Talk to me boys; I don't like to do much explaining. I need a girl who understands my needs, maybe some role playing."

CJ looked over at Mace then back at Javier, then said, "Princess is perfect for role playing. That's the newest girl in the house, and I'll tell you, she is making people fall in love. You'll love her too."

"New?" Javier asked. "She might not be open to role playing, maybe someone more seasoned."

"Papi," CJ said, "when I tell you she is a pro, I mean it. Mace trains these little bitches good. I haven't had the pleasure yet, but from the way I hear her clients through the halls, I know the pussy is good." He looked over at Mace. "I'm adding her to my personal list."

"You sound confident in this Princess," Javier said.

"I'm confident in everything I say, Javier."

"Well that's what we call a deal gentlemen. I'm getting rock hard just thinking about my money and my Princess.

This is why I come to you, you make fantasies real and well worth the flight."

◆◆◆◆

"Pow!" Kitty yelled, slamming her King and Ace on the table ecstatic to claim her winnings. "Give me my money." She sang while counting the chips Gigi slowly handed out.

Kitty, Gigi, Hannah and Yani were avid black jack players. There was a rush in taking each other's money, and when they couldn't get to the casino, they brought the casino to them. It was 1 AM in the house, and the group was on their fourth hour of playing. No less than $25 a hand, Kitty was slowly cleaning the crew out of their hard earned money.

"Deal again, I'm on a roll," Kitty said.

Gigi took on the role of the dealer and shuffled the deck. "Place your bets," Gigi yelled. She waved her hand over the table to bless it with luck, then placed the cards in front of each of the girls.

"Double down," Kitty said. The excitement was more then she could handle. With a flip of the top card, her palms sweated, and she hoped her hand would play out better than Gigi's.

"Black jack muthafuckas," Kitty yelled, bursting into laughter and doing the cabbage patch.

"What's that the funky chicken?" Yani said. "Sit your Asian ass down."

Kitty continued to dance. "Well my black side can play cards," she said, "and my Asian side can love long time, so I must be doing something right."

The group laughed at Kitty's silly behavior. Kitty was the little sister out the bunch. As pretty as she was she had the biggest sense of humor and made light of every situation. Just like Princess, shortly after graduation she was tricked by Ro to come to the house. She had been treated to an expensive trip to Miami, then forced to repay the money. Then after being allowed to go home to Texas, she quickly found her way back.

The oldest daughter of a Cambodian immigrant, she had responsibilities to take care of back at home and found the money that Ro provided as the best means. Her mother was living in poverty and her six little brothers and sisters needed to be cared for. Her father was a deadbeat, leaving her barely English speaking mother to fend for herself and seven children in a country made for college degrees. Laughter was the only stress reliever that she could find that wasn't toxic to her health.

"Deal me in," Princess said.

The girls got quiet at the sound of Princess's voice. Princess had been in the house for three weeks and had never attempted to join the girls in playing cards before. She usually remained in her bedroom until a client came around. She even ate in her room. Mace didn't allow her to take trips to the city with the other girls, and the only company she would see was Mace in the middle of the night, so the other girls' surprise at seeing her was understandable.

"Of course, Princess," Kitty said. "It's about time you came out of your cave." Kitty came and grabbed her arm and led her to a seat.

The girls sat around for another hour playing and joking. Princess didn't say much but still kept a smile on her face. She was tired and fought to keep her eyes open because she preferred playing cards to watching the clock, awaiting Mace's tap at the bedroom door. Slowly, she loosened up, and the girls' charming school girl attitudes were cheering her up. It was just what she needed.

"So what's Philly like, Princess?" Hannah asked.

Hannah's question sent butterflies to Princess's stomach. With a big sigh Princess reflected on memories of her childhood. All she'd thought about was home for the last few weeks and how she needed her old life back. Mace was becoming a monster and treated her like his personal sex slave. Finding thrills in sexual escapades and receiving compliments from strange men was becoming her only source of uplifting and an escape.

"Philly is cool. It's not glamorous like Miami, Cali, or Vegas. It damn sure ain't friendly like Texas or Alabama, but its home." Princess shrugged her shoulders while requesting a hit on her hand. "It's all the memories I have. My dad used to take me to Simon's ice skating rink when I was little, which was on the same field that the West Oak Lane Wild Cats football team played on, and was right behind my grandparent's house. But I cheer-leaded for the Mt. Airy Bantams, which was down the street from the house of my first boyfriend who was a starter on Germantown High school's football team. I never missed a homecoming game."

"Sounds like a small town," Yani said.

"Nah, nothing small about it. Philly is huge. That's just Uptown I'm referring too. The city has everything, and depending on what area you're in determines what you should expect. If you want to hit a bar and you're underage, go down North, if you want to find an after hour spot, hit up West."

"And what if you're looking for a house of queens?" Gigi said.

"I don't know much about whore houses in Philly, but I'm sure there are some."

"Well, Philly sounds cool, maybe we can hit up Mace's hometown one day and see what it's about. But in the meantime, black jack!" Kitty flipped over her cards and laughed hysterically.

"Princess," came the sound of Mace's voice from behind her.

The girls' eyes shot down to the cards in their hands. Mace stood with his icy stare fixed on Princess. Without hesitation Princess got up from the table and followed him to his bedroom.

"Sit down, Princess," Mace said, once they got to his room.

Princess sat on the edge of the king sized mattress biting her lip. A blow job or a hard fuck? Which task of their nightly routine she would have to perform first? Mace reached into his pocket, pulled out Princess's cellphone, and tossed it on the bed. Princess looked at the phone like it was a foreign object. It had been weeks since she had placed a call. She had forgotten all about the device. There had to be tons of missed calls and text messages.

"I need you to call home. Tell your parents you're okay and that you've been having so much fun that you can never find the right time to call, with the time difference and all. Tell them you found a part time job waitressing and you want to stay a little longer. Tell them that you *love* Vegas, the trees, the shopping, casinos, and the clubs, but you are going to come back to get some of your things. You just want to enjoy your rent free living a little longer before taking the flight back to Philly. They've been calling for you and I don't want them to think you're dead. I've been texting Kia on your behalf. She's good and knows that you're okay. I'm sure she's told your parents but—" He shrugged.

Princess picked up the phone and threw it across the room. Mace swiftly gripped a full hand of her hair, jerking her head back. He then yanked her head back and forth until she was eye to eye with him.

"I don't have time for the bullshit, Princess," he yelled, forcing her head around so she couldn't miss seeing the gun he had casually laying on the nightstand. Releasing his grip, his lips pressed against hers apologetically.

With tears in her eyes Princess made the call. Movies and books painted the scenes that she told her parents about. With little knowledge of Vegas, her answers were short and empty. Her parents warned her not to take too long coming back to Philly, but wanted her to take the time to find her place in life. They were proud of her and wanted to show support, little did they know.

Chills rippled through Princess's body as her fingertip hit the *end* button. She sat in deep thought, emotionless. The young, innocent female that had been so full of life and excitement was gone. There were no more parties with Kia, summers at the plateau, or trips to Haines Street for water ice. No Finnley ball games, shopping at King of Prussia Mall, or South Street struts. She was broken just as Mace needed her to be. Strong enough to carry on but not strong enough to fight back.

"Hey, Princess."

The flamboyant Hispanic man sang her name like a birdy on a spring morning. Princess held back her laughter with a big grin and wide eyes. His tanned physique and broad shoulders were ripped with muscles. He stood 6'2 and his long black hair was pulled into a tight ponytail. Silky strands of chest hair peeped out of the four opened buttons on his yellow shirt, which was tucked tightly into his package hugging tan slacks. He wore lots of gold jewelry and had lots of pizazz.

"Hey," Princess sang back, laughing to herself.

This one had to be a joke. Yani had warned Princess that this week's client would be a Mexican gangster and to be respectful. But unless he participated in dance gangs, like in Westside Story, she couldn't picture that.

"Princess, I heard you are good with pleasure." The man smiled while letting out a slight moan. "My name is Javier and I need to be pleased."

This would be interesting. It was only a matter of time before she was put onto one of the freaky clients the girls had been telling her about. Some had foot fetishes and some needed a good spanking, for Javier, she could only imagine.

"Yes baby. I love to pleasure my man." Princess fell right into her part. She was becoming good at acting and the reward was a nice payoff and sometimes an extra tip.

"Good. I've been craving something special I'm sure you can help me with." Javier winked at Princess. He dug into his over the shoulder bag and pulled out a 12 inch, thick, flesh colored, strap-on dildo. Princess almost gasped at the sight but managed to maintain her composure. Princess was confused and tried to analyze the situation. She was told he was a gangster, but she didn't know any homosexual gangsters at home. All she could conclude was that this was his escape. She would be helping him live out a lifestyle he probably couldn't participate in back in Mexico. Fulfilling this sex-capade could help her stacks to get even closer to her dream pot. Princess took the tool out of his hand and slowly slid her hand along the plastic shaft in a jerking motion.

"Mmmm, this could be fun." She smiled not wanting him to feel uncomfortable with his secret desire.

Javier began to wag his hips like a dog hungry for a snack. Preparing for action, she sat the strap-on on the bed, then quickly tied her hair into a tight bun and put on a tight white tank top. She wanted to look as masculine as possible.

"Prince, I want to taste you," Javier said.

Prince? Princess tried her best to stay in character, but seeing this oversized giant submit to her tiny frame was comical. Javier snatched the strap-on from the bed and tossed it to Princess. She adjusted the strap-on to fit and took on the role of Prince.

"Come here, papi, and show me how much you want to taste me."

Javier instantly dropped to his knees and took the head of the fake penis into his mouth. The vision was more than Princess could bare. She wasn't a man and the penis wasn't real, but Javier was so focused on performing fellatio that Princess forgot what was and wasn't real also.

"Yes, baby, yes!" Princess felt the strength of being the man and tugged for more power. She grabbed the back of his head and plunged the penis deeper into his throat causing him to gag. She let out a chuckle before she grabbed his ponytail and plunged in again. "You can't handle this dick?" She asked, recalling her own past incidences.

"Yes, I can handle, Prince," Javier convincingly chanted while forcing more saliva to drip from his mouth.

"No teeth, bitch, suck that shit right." Princess was loving the control. She grabbed his hair and shoved the penis deeper in.

"Sorry, papi, just tell me how you like it." Javier cupped his lips over his teeth and continued his sucking.

"No, I know what you really want." She pulled the dildo out of his mouth, then said, "Turn around and bend over." She yelled out.

Javier dropped his pants to his ankles and hopped onto the bed. Princess was so unfamiliar with the process that she was unsure where to insert. Seeing him bent over turned her off but she had a job to do. Closing her eyes, she pictured Javier was really Mace. The thought of causing him pain turned her arousal back up and made her want to waste no time. Princess smacked Javier on the ass, grabbed the head of the dildo, and dug into Javier's semi open asshole causing him to yell out in pleasure and pain.

While the girls were working, Mace was going over October's books and the pay deposits for himself, CJ, and Ro, that Yani had established. Everything appeared to be on point and the business looked promising for the upcoming 2012. After years of ass kissing and ego butting, his clients were becoming regulars and even used the mansion as a reason to vacation in Las Vegas.

Mace placed the information and stash into a safe built into his closet. He adjusted the books to fit properly, and as he did so, he came across a photograph that had almost adhered to the safe's floor. Peeling it from the bottom, mixed emotions swarmed him as he took a trip down memory lane.

2001

Lauren was waiting on Mace's bed, in the room Mace rented in Southwest Philly, watching Maury on T.V., and munching on a microwaved bowl of Ramen noodles, when Mace walked in the door.

"Look what I got, baby," Mace said.

Mace tossed City Blue bags onto the bed while playfully trying to hit her. Lauren opened the bags and pulled out a fly, pink terry cloth Rocawear set with matching pink, grey and white Bo Jacksons; and the skirt set, jersey dress, and two more short sets that he bought her. It was going to be a fly spring. Mace had his own bags of button up shirts and shorts, a few Rocawear suits, and two clean pairs of white Air force Ones. He knew his shopping habit needed to be cut back in order to keep his stacks going, but he had been in the mood for a small shopping spree.

"Mace, I love it. Thanks so much." Lauren, 19, smacked her boyfriend on the lips with a huge kiss.

"You know I got you. Anything for my future baby moms."

"You mean wife."

"Yea, whatever." He laughed, waving her off.

"L Boogie, you trying to go out tonight?" Mace asked.

Lauren frowned up her face. "Where Fridays?"

"Don't front on that sizzling chicken." Mace laughed knowing that was her favorite dish at the restaurant.

"Can we go somewhere else? My friends been telling me about their dudes taking them to Maggianos."

"Ya friend's dudes don't go shopping for them either. Maybe next week we'll hit that spot, Lil mama, but I need to budget after that shopping trip; okay? Plus you know it's gonna be popping at Fridays. We can hit up South Street when we're done." Mace kissed her on the forehead and she agreed.

The young lovers kicked it in the house preparing Mace's orders until date night began. Lauren watched as Mace used a kitchen scale to weigh ounces of marijuana. Although she never practiced the procedure herself, she had become a good student. Mace schooled her on how to pack a bag to make it look full, and how he could cheat the college kids or his white clients out of full ounces. Blacks were too cheap to spend their money on anything that didn't appear to be worth the price.

After separating his orders into sandwich bags, Mace packed the baggies into a Clorox wipes container. While Lauren got ready for their night out, he went to drop off a few packages to waiting customers.

Unfortunately, he didn't make it three blocks before he was pulled over by a police K-9 unit. The dog sniffed out the drugs in the Clorox wipes container he'd thrown on the backseat of the car.

Mace waited two weeks before his initial court date, and after the back and forth process he was eventually sentenced to a year in jail. That year felt like the longest year ever. But Lauren did her part to help it go by. A week didn't pass by that Mace didn't get a letter, receive a visit, or have money on his books. Not only had she been holding him down but she was also paying rent on the room they rented. He was proud of his girl. He had heard so many horror stories about chicks fleeing as soon as their man got locked up that he prayed every day that Lauren wouldn't do the same.

The one thing Mace didn't understand was how she could maintain everything. Lauren wasn't no dummy, but she damn sure wasn't a hard worker either. From what he could remember she never mentioned anything about a job early in his bid. When he would ask her how she was maintaining she would vaguely reply, "Odd jobs." Mace learned to drop the subject, not wanting to hear anything that would ruin their relationship.

Upon Mace's release everything was glitter and gold. Lauren had his car and crib ready, as well as some new gear and a cell phone. That cloud only lasted about a week before they fell off and reality set in. Mace couldn't take it anymore. She did too good of a job keeping his life together while he was down. Short bid or not, he needed answers. Early one morning while lying in bed he impulsively blurted out the question.

"What the fuck you been doin for this money, Lauren?"

Lauren simply stared at him, bit down on her lip, but she didn't say anything.

"Answer me," Mace said.

She frowned, turned her eyes away from his then back again. She looked afraid to answer and he believed he knew why.

"Answer me, Lauren," he said again.

"Answer what, Mace?"

"I know you heard me," he said. "What the fuck you been doing for this money."

He watched the tears pool in her eyes. He knew that face she was making, he had seen it before. She was on the verge of tears. She sighed deeply and the first tear fell from her eyes, made the long trek down her cheek before running off the side of her face. Finally, she opened her mouth to speak. He knew what she was going to say, knew exactly what he was going to hear; he just wanted to hear her say it. Then in a voice just above a whisper she said, "Tricking."

"Tricking?" There was no way she'd just say that. He had to have heard wrong. "Tricking?" he said again, this time a little louder. He studied her face; saw more tears were falling. She was nodding her head yes.

"Bitch." He jumped out the bed to hold back his urge to strangle her.

"Mace," she cried, "I'm sorry, but I did it for you. I did it for us; please understand."

He couldn't stop looking at her. She was a stranger. A fucking stranger. Crept into his house, ate his fucking porridge, slept in his fucking bed. He didn't even know the woman lying on the bed in front of him. His bed. A whore lying in his bed. He felt his own tear fall from his eye then. His precious Lauren was no better than any of the other hos he heard about in jail. She was worse.

"Ahhhh," He yelled. Then he slammed the 60 inch TV to the floor and left out of the room. If he hadn't seen the TV then it would've been Lauren.

It was three weeks before Mace returned to the box of a room and gave Lauren another chance. Staying with his mom and her new boyfriend wasn't the most comfortable place to stay, but it beat living with a whore. The only person he felt he could discuss the matter with was a friend he had made in jail. Leon was two decades older than Mace and was a true gangster. Mace had developed a bond with Leon, so Mace wrote Leon a letter explaining everything. When Mace received his letter from Leon he found that Leon had only written a few short sentences. "Stop working for your feelings," Leon wrote, "and find a way to make those feelings work for you. You always gotta be able to put your best girl on the block." With those words Mace returned home and had a talk with Lauren.

Mace sat and listened to Lauren describe how she had gotten in the game and how there was a lot of room for money. He couldn't fathom that his baby girl was now a turned out ho, but he listened with both ears and made Lauren feel comfortable. She went into detail on how she and her Jamaican friend, Isis, became regulars at Caribbean clubs and other foreign dancehalls. Because Isis's grew up around her father's Jamaican eatery, she often observed not only her father's friends but also other

Jamaican businessmen who came there to eat. So when she saw these same men in the clubs she often knew who was paid and who was fronting. Once she and Isis became known on the club scene, they began getting all kinds of monetary offers from the wealthy men who wanted a young doll to play with. They learned how easy it was to make quick money with foreigners and never turned tricks with American men again.

Mace liked the idea of dealing with foreigners and knew it was time to make a choice. And his only choice was to pimp out Lauren. At first, she hesitated at the idea; but after Mace convinced her he wouldn't do anything to harm her, she agreed. They both agreed to leave Isis out of the deal so their relationship wouldn't get destroyed by gossip and outside opinions. They were going to milk the cow together.

Somebody had lied, pimpin' was easy, but after three years of being in the game their relationship was completely destroyed. He no longer had love for Lauren. All he saw was money. Then one day Mace came home to their luxury apartment to find a letter stating she was leaving the state and to have a nice life. Her clothes were gone and so were any sign that she had ever lived in that house. Though he quickly replaced Lauren with other ho's, including her friend Isis, Mace never saw Lauren again.

Mace looked at the picture for a few more seconds before placing it back in the safe. It was amazing how much of a resemblance Princess had to Lauren. They both had the same creamy brown, naturally radiant skin, almond eyes that demanded your attention, full lips, and memorable smiles. He wanted Princess more now than ever.

Although Princess begged Mace to let her get some rest when he woke her out of her much needed slumber, he insisted he needed her more than she needed the rest. She reluctantly slipped on a pair of flip flops and did as she was told.

Mace led Princess outside to the pool. The desert air was cool unlike the blazing temperature any other time. She could hear the sounds of wild animals playing in their natural habitat. The bugs and other animal noises echoed even more now than during the day.

Mace took off all his clothes and eased himself into the pool. Princess stood with her arms crossed, hot with aggravation. Her body was far from her own. She had been having sex twice a day with two different men for some time now, and although it didn't bother him, it killed her. All of the health classes and pamphlets from doctor offices rang alarm bells in her head on the daily. She was being mentally tortured. Yes, she used condoms with her clients, but not with Mace. Every night she felt dirtier than the last and prayed for forgiveness.

"C'mon, Princess," Mace said. He reached his hand out for hers. Princess stared at him, with her arms still folded. "Princess, you're really testing my patience tonight. Hurry up and get in the pool."

Princess carefully stepped into the pool, walking deeper until the warm water reached her shoulders. Mace swam over to her and lifted her legs until she wrapped them around him. He licked her neck and pressed his body close to hers.

"Remember how we met?" Mace asked.

"Yes, Mace, how could I forget?"

"I told you I wanted to make your pussy famous, right? I have. Niggas all over the world know you got that good shit."

Was she supposed to feel proud? Inside she could see herself drowning his ass and enjoying watching him struggle for air until he died. She knew that would never happen, so all she could do was look away to hold back her desire for revenge.

"Mace, I'm tired. I really just want to sleep."

"I know, Princess, and you will get some, I promise. You're not enjoying this? I thought it would be nice to change the scene. Plus I wanted to feel you as wet as you could possibly get."

"No, I'm not enjoying this. I need some sleep."

"Okay."

Mace reached for his manhood and began fondling her for entry. Princess blocked her hole and let her legs fall from around his waist. Mace picked her legs back up and began his search again with more aggression.

"Why you always want to fight me, Princess?"

Mace found his way to the opening and squeezed her ribs with enough force to pull her body down allowing entry. Princess knew not to fight, or it would cause small rips inside of her which would make sex with her clients uncomfortable. Mace, as always, only concerned about himself continued to pump away.

Ro was the freshest big nigga Yani knew. Bitches loved the fly fat nigga's style, and today he'd arrived at the house for one of his monthly visits to check the books. Although Ro was a one third investor in the Vegas house, he had more money than both CJ and Mace. Yani knew from hearing him and CJ talk that Ro not only invested in the Vegas house, but also had girls working in Houston, and had his hands deep in the coke game there too.

She and CJ sat in CJ's room and waited for Ro to join them. When Ro walked into the room, he wasted no time getting started.

"Books is good?" Ro asked.

CJ took the thick accounting ledger from Yani's hands and handed it to him.

"Books are great," CJ said. "Look for ya self."

Even though Ro was something like a master accountant when it came to numbers, because Yani did the books, she had to stay until Ro checked each transaction one by one.

"So what's up?" CJ asked. "You at Texas, or Florida, after this trip?"

"After I get my money," Ro said, opening the ledger, "I'm back to Florida, to see my connect. Lots of money to be made in coke, CJ. You got enough dough to ski. When you going to be ready to play in the snow?"

"Nah, you going to deep. I'm cool where I'm at, Ro."

Yani knew the only reason CJ didn't get involved in the drug game was because he thought by not getting down she was safer. And maybe he was right? Still, every time Ro came for his visit he made CJ the same offer.

"What's up with the girls?" Ro asked, eyes glued to the ledger.

"Still ho'n," CJ said.

"And Mace's new little bitch?"

CJ shot Yani a look as if to tell her to keep her mouth shut. Yani shrugged.

"What about her," CJ said.

Yani was sure Ro heard the tension in CJ's tone, just as she had, because he immediately looked up from the ledger.

"Is there something I need to know about, Lil' homie?" Ro asked.

CJ let out a nervous chuckle. "Why you say that?"

Ro sat the ledger down and stared at CJ. "CJ, what's up with Mace's new bitch?"

CJ sighed. "Exactly what you said, Mace's bitch."

Yani inhaled sharply, surprised her cousin said even that much after the look he gave her.

Ro frowned at her, then asked CJ, "What does that mean?"

"What's already understood don't need no explanation; do it, pimpin'?"

Ro's eyes narrowed and Yani could tell he was thinking through CJ's statement. He then nodded and smiled. "Yea, I hear you, Lil' homie. But you ain't got to worry about Mace. I'm sure he's just having fun with something new. He knows how the game goes."

2010

Kesh fixed her blazing red hair as the curls bounced down to the tip of her shoulders. She was admiring her own beauty in the mirror. The vanity mirror's light bulbs highlighted her green contacts. They made the perfect accessory to her freshly tanned skin thanks to the generous Miami sun. Eager to do some late night sun bathing, Kesh tightened the straps on her gold stilettos and fixed the cups on her white thong bikini top. With one last rub down of baby oil she was ready to hit Ocean Drive.

Just like any other day in Miami tourist filled the streets half drunk, half high, and all the way ready to party. She pranced down the street to Mango's, a hot Caribbean restaurant known for it's beautiful waitresses, and bartenders who dressed more like exotic dancers. Her friend Selena was a   bartender at the hot spot. Although Kesh was slowly making money with the modeling scene, she was hoping Selena could land her a waitressing job at the restaurant.

Kesh entered Mangos and made her way straight for the bar. Her friend Selena saw her and came over after serving a customer his drink.

"So what did your boss say about the job?" Kesh asked.

"Well," Selena said, "I have some good news and bad news." Selena frowned as she mixed a Margarita, for a customer. "My boss isn't in today but he does want to meet you. I told him how you've been modeling in the clubs and that you would be a great addition to the team. I explained to him how building your buzz can work both ways and he loved the idea."

"Thanks, Selena." Kesh appreciated the help even though she was hoping to start work immediately.

"On another note," Selena said, "we have a hot date tonight."

"With who?" Kesh asked.

"Some guys I met last night. They said they want to hit the beach tonight with some drinks before they head out."

"Sounds like fun as long as they have transportation. I promised myself, no more dates with tourist who use mopeds to get around. I need style."

"Nope, they have that and more. Trust me."

A few hours later, Kesh prepared for her and Selena's night out on the beach. A shiny gold bathing suit with gold hoop earrings and a black sheer wrap to hug her hips was the perfect choice to dazzle in the moonlight and more than anything her red hair would be an eye catcher.

When the doorbell rang, Kesh kissed her mother on the cheek and headed to the front door, praying for a halfway decent looking date. She was certain he would be the opposite, like most men she met. To her surprise, when she opened the door, a honey brown skinned brother with the most perfect set of teeth she had ever seen stood there. She peeked her head out the door, looking for Selena. Her friend was grinning from ear to ear next to her own date. They were about to be escorted around the city in a shiny black Mercedes Benz with tint so dark the windows blended right into the car door. That was something to smile about. Personally, Kesh would've liked it better if the car didn't have tint so she and Selena could've been seen looking so lavish.

If her date was as paid as he appeared to be, she wanted to make a great impression. Although she knew there were a lot of fake ballers in Miami, he appeared to be the real thing.

"Hello," Kesh said, greeting the handsome man with a kiss on the cheek. "I'm Sky." As was her custom when meeting new people, she gave him her modeling name.

"Mace," he said.

On the way to the beach everyone laughed and joked while enjoying puffs of marijuana. Kesh was surprised at how affectionate Selena was being with his friend Ro. She rubbed Ro's round tummy while laughing and hanging on to his every word. Money or no money he didn't seem like Selena's type.

Mace complimented Kesh on her sexy accent and at how naturally striking she was. Kesh teased Mace telling him to show her and not tell her how he felt while tickling his pant leg.

The beach was filled with romance as the couples sipped champagne, and then played in the temperate ocean. Mace was making Kesh feel totally at ease in the gentle ebb and flow of the ocean's current. He held her close and they kissed passionately. Kesh just wanted to enjoy the night before he had to go home to Philly. If you asked her, she was finally experiencing what it felt like to be swept off her feet.

Mace didn't have to spend a lot of money to gain Kesh's attention like some of the others. His charm, good looks, and soft yet masculine touch created creamy juices in her bikini bottom. And she could tell Mace's sexual attraction to her was through the roof as well. He fed her the champagne as she sucked on the rim of the bottle like a cherry lollipop. "Mmmm," Kesh moaned. She was utterly intoxicated and frisky.

"Let me see, Sky," Mace said, opening her toned thighs to get a grip on her hardened clit. Kesh shivered as her garden pulsed and ejected cream onto his hand. She had been dying to feel his touch. Mace kissed her lips and squeezed tighter causing her to bend over in pleasure.

"Relax, mama, not in the ocean," He said, chuckling.

"Where are you staying?" she asked.

"The Chateau," he said.

Both knew what time it was. They pushed through the gentle current and gathered their items on the beach. Ro and Selena had long since disappeared into the hotel. By the time they made it to Mace's luxurious suite, she couldn't wait to strip down and taste him.

First, they took a steamy hot shower. Mace looked like a Men's Magazine cover model. As the water splashed and coursed down his chest and abs creating a centerfold shot; Kesh released a waterfall of her own. Her vagina, warm and hot, trickled her sweet juices as her manicured nails danced in and out of her walls. She squatted down in front of Mace with her knees spread wide apart. Mace rang a rag over her shoulders causing suds to cascade over her breast and down to her vagina. Aroused by the vision of her own breast covered with suds, she grabbed Mace's penis, put it in her mouth, then began working her lips up and down on his pulsing manhood, enjoying it's fresh warm taste. She could feel the hot tension of Mace's penis against her tongue and knew he was close to orgasm. Before he could cum, she slowly pulled him out of her mouth and kissed the tip.

"Get up," he said.

Kesh stood up and Mace pushed down on her back so he could shove his thickness inside her. Kesh screamed for mercy as Mace banged against her wide hipped round ass. Mace was pounding so hard she started to lose her breath. Water was suffocating her while flowing over her hair and over her face, but she wasn't about to tell him to stop.

"Ahhhh, damn, Sky," Mace cried, as Kesh's warm milk poured onto his meat and he squirted hot semen into her throbbing vagina.

A few hours after their exhausting love making session, Kesh and Mace were knocked out cold, when suddenly, she was awakened by a tapping sound. She peered through one eye at the hotel door. When she heard the tapping sound again, she figured some drunken tourist had mistaken Mace's hotel room for their own. She cautiously peeled back the covers so as to not disturb Mace, who was still asleep, and tiptoed to the door. When she opened the door, she found Selena standing there frantically waving for her to step into the hallway.

"What's wrong, Selena?" Kesh began panicking and immediately assumed Ro had hurt her friend.

"Let's switch," Selena said, referring to sex partners.

"Hell no, bitch." They had done it once before but this would not be a repeat of that night.

Selena grinned, pulled out a wad of cash, and said "Then, chica, we got to go."

"Did Ro give you that?" Kesh said.

"No. So if you know like I know, it's time to leave."

Kesh's face turned as red as her hair. She had finally met a man that sent chills through her body, and Selena pulls this kind of stunt? She wanted nothing more than to nestle in Mace's arms and to greet him with a sweet breakfast from room service. Had she known what her friend intended, she would've told her to back off. She had a genuine connection with Mace, but Selena never considered that. She was too busy being focused on the typical Miami woman's hustle.

"Bitch," Selena said, "we have to go, and now."

Kesh knew Selena was right. Her friend was not about to plant the money back in Ro's pocket, and Kesh damn sure didn't want to get caught with it in their possession.

"Okay," Kesh said, then turned away from Selena and slid back into the room.

Sly as a fox, Kesh moved throughout the room gathering her bag, shoes, and bathing suit bottom. She was wearing Mace's t-shirt so she decided to wear it out of the hotel and disregarded her hoop earrings on the floor next to Mace's side of the bed. He fidgeted a bit from the little noise she did create but never fully woke. Kesh dressed in the hallway and caught up to the scandalous Selena who was outside flagging down a cab with the money she stole from Ro.

Kesh's eyes snapped open. She was alone in bed, her body was still aroused from the dreamy memory of Mace's body being against hers. She reflected on how never found the courage to tell Mace that she was Sky. Everything would've been perfect if it wasn't for the gold digging Selena. Love at first sight would've worked out in her favor. Due to the bitterness she felt, she stopped speaking to Selena once she found out she was pregnant by Mace. Mace could've been her chance to have a real family. Although she had none of his contact information she refused to abort his seed. She knew in her heart they'd one day meet again.

Unfortunately, her fantasy was short lived after miscarrying the baby during one of her waitressing shifts at Mangos. Blood seeped through her scantily clad clothing for everyone in the restaurant to see. She had been feeling sick the entire shift but needed the money and refused to go home even after being told to do so by the manager. Embarrassed and furious with her friend, she eventually headed for the fast cash of stripping to boost her modeling career. When Mace appeared in the club a year later, she just knew that God was granting her wishes. Only, Mace didn't recognize the newly blonde vixen without her green contacts and red hair. He approached her as if it was their first encounter. Perhaps too many one night stands blurred the vision that he obviously didn't share with her, but that didn't stop Kesh from wanting him. Plus, she couldn't tell him she was Sky or about the baby thanks to her good friend Selena. When Mace offered her the opportunity to work for him she jumped at the chance.

Kesh removed her fingers from her kitten and allowed some of the built up pressure to subside. Then she sat up on her elbow and reached over to the nightstand beside the bed and opened the top drawer. The 12 inch dildo sitting, atop the rest of her assortment of toys was exactly what she needed. She grabbed the dildo, laid back down, and fantasized about Mace while using the rubber penis to trace the outline of her face and moistened lips before she was overcome by another spicy desire.

Kesh reopened the nightstand drawer and pulled out the fake vagina she often used as a form of foreplay with her clients. She placed the vagina on the bed, then got on all fours, her ass propped in the air, and used her tongue to make small strokes on the fake pussy. Like a cat lapping up milk, she flicked her tongue up and down, growing more intense with every lick. Meanwhile she used one hand to rub the dildo up and down her aching walls. Wet with her juices, Kesh aggressively dug the dildo into the toy vagina.

"You like Princess's pussy; huh, Mace?" she said, growing hotter with anger. A movie of a thrilling night shared by Princess and Mace played in Kesh's mind. Kesh watched at eye level, dipping the dildo in and out of the fake pussy with growing excitement. "Is it better than mine?" she said.

"Hell no," she yelled, snatching the dildo out of the fake pussy and swatting the fake pussy to the floor. She then rolled over onto her back and penetrated her own vagina until she brought herself to climax.

CHAPTER TWELVE

As time passed in Mace's mansion, sleep was becoming harder to come by for Princess. Between long evenings with clients, nights with Mace, and her own anxiety levels building, Princess's sleep only came in sporadic increments. Late nights and early mornings, she would find herself waking up at 4:30 a.m. after going to bed at 2 a.m. She would hit the sack again around 10 a.m., once she could no longer keep her eyelids open, and sleep until hunger forced her to get up for food.

Eating was another habit getting lost in the mix. Princess was only devouring about one good meal a day, obsessed with keeping a good figure for her clients. A good figure meant good pay. The more money that poured in, the more she desired to keep her pockets fattened. Lots of coffee and lots of water filled her stomach and curbed her hunger until dinner arrived.

Finding herself in another sleepless mood at 3:30 a.m., Princess fumbled around the kitchen cabinets in search of some creamer. *Where the hell did they move it?* She needed it for the coffee she intended to make. The caffeine settled her anxiety and gave her a relaxing sensation that helped her jittery nerves. She moved on to the refrigerator. After she adjusted the refrigerated items, she found the hazelnut creamer mixed in with the yogurts and an immediate sense of calm swept over her.

Behind her, she heard the heavy foot falls of a man enter the kitchen. She rolled her eyes. There was no privacy in this house, and no opportunity to have even a moment without Mace hovering around. She ignored his approaching presence and pulled the coffee machine from the cabinet and sat it on the countertop.

"What are you doing up so early?" he said. The down south accent caught Princess completely by surprise.

Princess half turned and said, "Oh, CJ, I didn't expect you to be behind me. I thought it was Mace."

CJ laughed and Princess realized it was the first time she had ever seen him do so. CJ was usually quiet and mysterious. He often walked around lit up from weed or alcohol, but always seemed to handle the other girls with care. Princess wondered why the other girls warned her not to mess with him. Mace was the real monster, CJ was more like a minion, in her eyes.

"Make me a cup," CJ said. He went and sat down at the kitchen's round marble table while Princess retrieved two coffee mugs from the overhead cabinet.

After she filled the coffee machine, she joined CJ at the table and the two sat in silence as the strong aroma permeated the kitchen. CJ, his eyes glued to her, tucked his arms across his sculpted chest. Princess tried to ignore his stare. She could tell he was taking her measure. Princess fiddled with her nails in hopes that the machine's alarm would buzz soon, but the timer seemed like it was running on eternity. Curious about CJ's thoughts, Princess figured she might as well spend the next few minutes in a Q&A session.

"What?" she asked, cutting her eyes at him with a smile.

"You," he said.

"What about me?" It was feeling like a high school flirting session, and she was enjoying the game.

CJ rested his elbows on the table and rested his chin on top of his knuckles. His blonde dreads draped his hands as he looked up at Princess with a smile. Turning away from his sultry green eyes, Princess smiled. At the table was one of the sexist men she had ever seen, bare chested in a pair of Polo pajama pants. She knew he was off limits so there was no use in anymore teasing.

"You've been in this house for a while," CJ said, "and I've never gotten a chance to kick it with you. If we were back home, you'd be something to look at."

"Yea, well we're not." Princess said.

"Chill, shorty, nobody disrespecting you, just saying you a cutie. Pour my cup."

She stood from the table and went to the coffee machine. After mixing their concoctions, she returned to the table, handed CJ his mug, then sat back down with her own.

"So, what are you doing up so early?" he asked.

Princess took a sip of her coffee, "I can't sleep, CJ, I can never sleep."

"Not even with all that good-good you getting all day and all night?" He asked, smiling.

Princess didn't return the gesture. "It's not that good," she said.

"Which? The day or the night?"

"This just ain't me, CJ, this ain't my life. No disrespect to what yall have going on. I'm just not that girl."

"What kind of girl? You don't like being around powerful men, money makers, the real shakers of the world?"

Princess's eyes shot to CJ's. She had no answers to his questions.

"You don't like getting paid and putting in no real time? You don't like living with no responsibilities and no financial obligations? What can we do to make you not only like but *love* this lifestyle, Princess."

His words didn't hit her ears hard like Mace's usually did. CJ spoke like a boss that truly cared about his employee's. He had pointed out the bonuses of being a prostitute in such a way that any argument she posed would seem faulty.

"See the problem, Princess?" He slid the barstool from underneath him and moved closer to Princess. "You haven't learned how to control the situation."

Princess followed CJ's movements with her eyes. She tried to anticipate his words and actions, but CJ surprised her. As he spoke to her he kneeled down like a daddy speaking to his little girl.

"Don't be a victim," he said. "When you are in the room you need to control those men. Men love to be controlled. Once you master that, you can control everything else in your life. When that man enters your room, study him. Watch how he moves, what he looks at, see what grabs his attention. Say more with your body language and speak less words. Once you master that, he won't have to say much because, you can read him like a book. Do you understand?"

Princess nodded her head but wasn't quite sure she knew what he meant. How could she say more by speaking less? He kept calm and spoke slow to her, she was missing that kind of sincerity.

"Princess, you're doing good here, and I know that's why Mace is so afraid to let you go. Don't let that get to you, okay?" His calm manner and sincere tone made him easy to agree with, and she found herself nodding once again. "Command every situation," he said, standing, "and you will always be the victor." He reached out a hand and stroked her hair. "There's so much in you that I can see, Princess, you just have to see it too."

At that point he leaned in and kissed her on the forehead. An act so full of gentleness and affection she became lost in the moment. She reached for the hand he was stroking her hair with and interlaced her fingers with his. This time when CJ leaned in to kiss her, he pressed his plush pillows against her cheek, then whispered in her ear, "Command attention from your men, Princess."

Kesh was on her way to spy on Princess and Mace when she came across CJ and Princess in the kitchen. After two minutes of spying and seeing their close interactions, she decided to alert Mace. She went back to her room, got her cell phone, and shot Mace a text message as she continued to peep Princess's intimate coffee break through the crack in her bedroom door.

Hey, papi. I know I should not speak, but I'm really tired, and you and the misses chatting in the kitchen are keeping me up.

She hoped he would read the text. She gleefully waltzed to her bed and settled in. Even if he didn't see it tonight, the message would still leave his mind baffled and Princess would be in a heap of trouble. She felt closer to her throne.

Once Mace got to the kitchen, he fully understood Kesh's text. He saw CJ with one hand on Princess's cheek and his lips brushing against her ear.

"I wasn't invited to the morning tea?" Mace said.

CJ froze, then stood straight, removed his hand from Princess's cheek, and chuckled. "Nigga," CJ said, "you know everybody's invited when it comes to Princess."

"Well I didn't get the letter." Mace said, striding across the kitchen in their direction. CJ backed away from Princess, and Mace took CJ's place, stopping directly in front of her. "Why you ain't tell me about the party, Princess?"

Princess closed her eyes and shook her head. Mace wasn't surprised. She knew she had no business allowing CJ that close to her. There was no way he would tolerate that kind of behavior from her. She needed to learn a memorable lesion.

"Princess, did CJ pay you for some pussy?"

When Princess looked in CJ's direction, his irritation with her only increased. "Are you ignoring me, Princess?"

"Mace, I didn't do anything," she yelled.

Mace raised one eyebrow. "We yell now?"

"No."

"Sounded like yelling to me."

Princess rolled her eyes.

"I told you," Mace said, "1 catch eyes."

He then grabbed Princess by the face and shoved her head back. The unexpected force of the motion knocked both Princess and the barstool she was sitting on to the kitchen floor.

Mace shot a glance at CJ to see if he had anything to say about his actions. CJ scratched his head and looked away. Mace then looked back to Princess who looked like she was about to cry.

"Go to my room, Princess." Mace said.

With tears falling down her cheeks Princess quickly gathered herself from the floor and left the kitchen. Mace turned to CJ with a handshake. There was no way he could've let Princess get loud in front of one of his soldiers. Mace knew that CJ was coming on to Princess, but hos were gonna be hos, and he damn sure wasn't about to make business personal.

"Business is always business, CJ, you understand? Next time you want to fuck one of my bitches, I need five stacks." He released CJ's hand and exited the kitchen.

CHAPTER THIRTEEN

Topless, Princess decided to pull the already taut Velcro straps, that looped around the metal bar fixed between the bathroom doorway, a little tighter. In response, Jung, the naked, pale Japanese man whose wrist were secured above his head by the end of those straps, rose up on his toes. Princess nodded her head in satisfaction then traced her pink fingernails from one of Jung's shoulders to the other and giggled when she saw him shiver from her touch. Tucked under her arm was a hard wooden paddle which she took hold of and lightly tapped Jung on the ass. When she saw his body tense up at the slight contact, she dropped to her knees, secured the Velcro straps around his ankles, and quickly pulled the other end of those straps until Jung's body hung suspended in midair.

"I want to hear you scream," Princess said.

Jung looked over his shoulder with an incredulous expression and said, "I want to hear *you* scream."

For his lack of respect, Princess paddled him. "I said I want to hear you scream, Jung. You don't make mama scream, she makes you scream. Do you understand, baby?" Her question was met with a stubborn silence.

Princess grew agitated with his refusal to role play and decided she needed to embarrass him. His cocky attitude was no match for her paddle. She was not impressed with his money or celebrity. Tons of money makers flowed through her castle on the weekly basis, and they were looked at like workers at Walmart, nothing out of the ordinary. Most weren't as young as Jung, so she should've anticipated the problem that was occurring. Coming to the mansion wasn't even his idea. Jung's manager Paul, who was a frequent client of Hannah's whenever he came to the states had paid for his visit. Jung was used to regular shit with regular bitches, bitches that cared to make him feel like a man. Princess was determined to make him feel lower than he had ever felt.

"Mmmmm Jung," Princess moaned while grabbing her nipples.

Jung let out a moan.

"I thought you wanted to try something different?" Princess said.

"Princess, I never—"

"Sshhh."

"Princess, I don't know—"

"Sshhh," Princess reached for his nipples and proceeded to twist.

"Ahhhh!" Jung screamed.

Princess looked up with excitement. "Is that what you call screaming, Jung?" She said, "I think you can do better than that."

Princess puckered her lips to give him a kiss then, before their lips could meet, Princess smacked his red ass once again. Whap!

He looked at her in a panic. "Okay, Princess, okay."

"I said scream!" She wacked him once again, using more strength than she had before.

"Ahhhhhh! Princess! Ahhhhhhhh!"

Although Jung dropped his head back and let out a scream that was satisfactory to Princess's dominatrix persona, she wanted more. Five more hardcore paddles to Jung's backside and he screamed in defeat.

"You like it, Jung?" she asked, whispering into his ear.

For a moment he was silent, then in a barely audible voice, he said, "Yes, I like it."

"I know you do," Princess said, as she reached around to the front of his pelvis and caressed his rock hard penis.

Instantly, Princess slid underneath his hoisted body and began performing the sloppiest fellatio. She knew leaving her client feeling pleased after his paddling was a must, and a feeling he would never forget.

♦♦♦♦

"Make sure you close the door tight, Yani," Princess said in a low tone. Yani went back to the door and pushed it harder to assure it's closure. Princess sat crossed legged in her leopard chair; her thinking chair. It was her personal corner to drift and dream as she mapped out her involvement in the house. She knew that Mace felt a special bond with her, but she didn't know why. What she did know was that her time in the house was running short. You can only chain a beast for so long before it found a way to break free, and when it did, you'd better watch out for it's bite.

Princess rested her head on the back of the chair. "Yani, he's winning and I've never been a loser."

"I know, Princess. He needs you and he cares for you. Trust me, he just doesn't know how to express it."

"Fuck that! You must think I'm stupid."

"No, Princess, really, Mace is in love with you. He's a pimp, Princess, all he knows is control. He controls women. But he cares for you, you best believe that. That's why he is so afraid to let you go. He feels a connection with you that he doesn't feel with the rest of the girls. Didn't he just buy you a necklace?"

"So?" Princess snatched the platinum chain with an iced out "P" from the nightstand and tossed it in Yani's lap. "Take that shit and pawn it."

"Princess."

"Yani, are you serious right now? That nigga don't love me. How could you even say that? Are you serious? You must be brainwashed or something. You think this is life?"

"So what, Princess?"

"Mace has me making weekly phone calls to my cousin and family with a gun held to my face. Does he do that to you? No. I know that you volunteered for this shit, but I didn't. I'm done, Yani."

Yani wore a doubtful expression on her face. "So what are you going to do about it?"

"No," Princess said, "what are *you* going to do about it?"

"Me?"

"Yes, you. Yani." Princess shot daggers at Yani like it was her obligation to make a move. "Your time here is almost up. I need you to get me and all the other girls home with you. We can do this shit on our own and make mad dough." Princess snapped her fingers in Yani's puzzled face.

"So you don't want to be done with tricking, you just don't want to trick for Mace?"

"Nah, I'm done with this shit. But I can run it— we can run it. Setup our own house; get our own clients; fuck it, we can make the other girls work for us but give them a bigger pay that will make them want to leave this house."

Princess had been thinking of her plan for some time. She wasn't sure if college would still be on her agenda after seeing how much money she could make so easily. It would take a lot of courage, but she figured she had learned a lot by being so close to Mace. Nothing was impossible.

"You think that we'll set up shop in Nevada and still live?"

"Why do we have to be in Nevada?" Princess asked.

"Princess, what are you saying? Come to me when you have a real plan because right now you're just talking shit."

"I'm not, Yani. I sit here everyday in my chair and think. After the clients and dealing with Mace all I can do is think."

"So basically you're going crazy?"

"Yes, but I haven't lost it. Listen, we're gonna rob these niggas and start our own shit. But I need y'all help. Mace has a ton of dough in his room and I can get to that, you can get to CJ's, and somehow we can get to Ro's. We can take that money and buy our own house, and work on getting our own clients. Hell we can take some of theirs. Since you're leaving the house, we can pay the driver to take all of us to the airport and get ghost."

"So you want to rob Mace? That's definitely something I didn't expect to hear from you." Yani chuckled and shook her head. "You must be damn near suicidal to even think of something like this. Mace must've really pushed you to the edge."

Yani quieted for a moment, then said, "You do understand if we do this, and they find us, they'll kill us? And what are we supposed to do about the driver? You think he won't tell?"

"If he snitches, he'll be a dead man anyway just for taking us. So if he knows like I know, he will get ghost too. Toss him like 40 g's and tell him to start his own driving service. Fuck it, he can come too."

"What makes you think he'll be down? He might have a family or something."

"Well next time you go into town ask him. Spark conversation about his life. C'mon Yani, you do this every day to get info out of your clients; a man is a man. You have a few trips to make into the city before this goes down. Get to know him. Don't give him anything to think about just in case he's a snitch. On your last night, as he's loading the bags, pass him the money and tell him the deal. He won't have a choice, and the paper will look good in his hands."

Yani slowly nodded. "It could work." She paused. "But I'm not robbing my cousin, Princess, that's out. Pimp or no pimp, that's fam."

"Fine," Princess said. "We can focus on Mace and Ro." Princess shrugged it off.

"No, Princess. I can't leave CJ hanging like that. Either he needs to be in on this, or— he just needs to be in on it, okay. So if you really want my help with this plan of yours, you need to think of some way to include my cousin."

How she would pull CJ into the plan was beyond her. This was his house too. But CJ would have to be incorporated if Yani was going to help, and she needed Yani.

"Alright, I'll think about it, and you think about how you're going to break the news to the other girls. They trust you, you're the vice president in this thing. If you don't make them believe you, then they damn sure won't believe me; got it?"

"One thing at a time, Princess. Handle my cousin; got it?"

Princess grinned. She would handle CJ all right. She just needed more time to think.

CHAPTER FOURTEEN

Saturday

Club Jag as always was packed with people, and the musky smell of cigars and sweat filled the air. The laser lights raced around the inside of the club while the pole dancers showed off their hottest moves. Mace held tight to Princess's hand as the house members swarmed the VIP. It was exactly what she needed. The change of scenery was well deserved and the perfect outlet for her frustrations. Princess sipped on long island iced teas as she winded her hips to the sounds of reggae. She looked like a fly girl in her long sleeved form fitting black dress and platinum bamboo earrings, and her "P" chain glistened as the lasers hit it. With her hair pulled into a long ponytail all of her features, especially her bright red lipstick, stood out.

Mace walked Princess around the velvet roped section, arm in arm, as he met with different entertainers and business men. The club was really a networking opportunity for the haves, versus it being a party scene for the have nots. After making his rounds and setting up a few transactions, Mace hung onto Princess like a child on his mother's hip.

He stared at her with glassy eyes and said, "You know you're a star right, Princess?"

"That's what you say, Mace." Princess winked at him and squeezed his hand.

Mace rushed Princess with a hug that almost toppled her over. He planted a rough kiss on her cheek as he grabbed her waist ready to dance.

"Nice chain, Princess," Kesh yelled into Princess's ear.

Princess looked down at the necklace with the P piece that had lain forgotten against her chest until Kesh mentioned it. Kesh reeked of liquor, and Princess knew the girl was high off some of the joints they rolled in the limo. She also knew Kesh was jealous. The girl seemed to think Princess was in a position to be proud of, but for all Princess cared, Kesh could've had Mace however she wanted him. She ignored Kesh's sarcastic little statement, but Kesh was persistent.

"You must've sucked *a lot* of dick to earn that piece," Kesh said.

Princess laughed off Kesh's verbal jab, grabbed the necklace and flashed the P piece in Kesh's face. "Trust me Kesh, it was definitely the power of the P."

"Bitch, you are the weakest link, that's why Mace uses you like he does," Kesh said.

Princess glanced at Mace, saw he was purposely ignoring her and Kesh's growing argument, and said, "Just as weak as that float your ass came to this country on."

Kesh reached out and grabbed Princess's ponytail. Princess tried to swing on Kesh but Mace lifted her into the air by her waist and demanded for Kesh to let her go. Kesh instantly let go of Princess's hair and laughed.

"Bitch," Princess yelled, "wait till we get back to the house." Mace held her in the air while she frantically swung her arms trying to break from his hold. CJ grabbed Kesh by the arm and drug her out the door.

Yani, pumps in hand, rushed out of the club to the limo where she saw CJ hunched over Kesh who sat with her feet still outside the limo. CJ's fingers were wrapped around Kesh's jaw like she was a child.

"I don't give a fuck what happened," Yani heard CJ saying to Kesh, "we have clients, and there are cops all around the club. You know better than this. Now don't get out of this limo; you understand?"

Yani heard Kesh utter something unintelligible, then CJ straightened up and Kesh pulled her feet inside the limo and sat back.

"Yo, CJ," Yani said, "what happened?"

CJ looked over his shoulder at his cousin, shook his head, slammed the limousine's door, then turned around. "This bitch is tripping, fighting in the club and shit."

Yani played as if she didn't already know, and said, "Who was she fighting? Princess? Why?"

"Stupid shit. Listen, I gotta check up with Mace and watch the other bitches. Keep your eye on her and make sure she don't come back in. I gotta finish talking to my peoples." CJ walked off leaving Yani to babysit.

Yani put her face close to the limousine's window and peered inside, Kesh was laid back inhaling a joint. *How did I become a babysitter?* She walked up to the passenger side window and tapped on the glass.

"Julio." The chubby, thick-mustached driver cracked the front window just enough to hear what she had to say. "Can I sit in the front?" Yani asked. "I have to watch Kesh, but I really don't feel like being around that bitch. My feet hurt and I need to sit."

Julio unlocked the door. Yani climbed into the front seat and relaxed her aching feet. The back of the limo was different from the driver's compartment. She noticed the buildup of cigarette butts in the ashtray and how little room there was up front. It was clear Julio spent a lot of time in the limo. The seats were worn out, and there were old junk food wrappers that hadn't been thrown out, but here she was. Everything happened for a reason, right?

Yani thought about her next move, then said, "So, Julio, how long have you lived in Vegas?"

CHAPTER FIFTEEN

Sunday

"Did you start working on your plan for CJ yet?" Yani said. She sat on Princess's bed with her legs crossed, shaking her foot back and forth.

Princess wasn't thinking about CJ at all. She was still heated about the previous night's events but was warned not to fight Kesh. Mace wasn't having a house of chaos, and she knew that if anyone would be punished for fighting, it would be her. Princess just added the situation with Kesh as one more reason to fuck over Mace.

"Well, Julio is originally from Mexico, but moved to Nevada after living in Arizona for a few months. He has a wife and three kids in Mexico that he sends money to over there."

"Yani, how did you find that out?"

"While you were busy getting your cat on, I was clawing for info." The two laughed, the southern belle's accent always tickled Princess's ear with amusement.

"Well good. He can take his ass right back. That's perfect, Yani, 40 g's is more than enough for him to be comfortable in Mexico. Maybe he won't find any clients to drive in a limo, but I'm sure he can start a taco stand or something."

"Well, you need to figure out what are you're going to do about CJ," Yani said.

"Don't worry," Princess said, "I got a plan." She wasn't lying either, she did have a plan, it just wasn't fully worked out.

"Well, when you're ready I'm here to listen."

"Just get the girls together for a pool side lunch on Friday," Princess said.

"Friday? Why so long?"

"I just have a feeling we won't be able to talk about it until then."

Mace stretched across his king sized mattress and watched the time go by on his bedroom clock. The big bed, cushioned with fluffy, black satin pillows, felt empty. As tough as he was, there was nothing like the feeling of a warm body in bed next to his. After Saturday's spat in the club he decided to cool things down by keeping Princess away. Kesh was his money maker, and even though he knew how to check her, unnecessary stress could be avoided. Allowing Kesh to feel like she won was a small price for him to pay in order to keep attitudes down and money at a high. He knew Kesh's jealousy had grown but didn't know it had grown enough to attack Princess. Truth be told, after the altercation between her and Princess, he wanted to have sex with Kesh more than ever. There was something sexy about her wanting him bad enough to fight over him that fed his ego. Even before the fight she had been finding ways to entice him whenever she found him alone. Flirty moments accompanied with sweet touches to make his dick stand at attention were becoming more frequent. She would even offer to pole dance in his room to help him get ready for Princess.

The few times Kesh stripped for him, she would finish her show with a sloppy blow job that would end right before he would nut. She was built to be a Queen. Any regular man would be weak for her dime quality looks and her sex appeal. With them, if she wanted it, she would have it, and that was exactly what she was used to. Kesh thought she could come up by being his bottom bitch. She was out for money and power but Mace wasn't about to give up either to a gold diggin ho with a spicy mean streak.

He began thinking about the times Kesh performed her sexy moves, and he rubbed the bulge forming in his boxers. Would he need her tonight? Yes, allowing Kesh to dance for him would be the perfect way to make her feel relevant while curbing his own sexual needs. Sitting up to roll a blunt he laughed to himself about the cat fight that had occured. He still had it. Reminiscing on his younger days when females would be out in the streets, banging on his door for his old girl Lauren to come outside to catch a beat down. There was something gratifying in women fighting over a good piece of dick, something to be proud of.

Mace picked up his phone to give Kesh a call but decided against it. She was the only girl in the house that was allowed to have a phone because he knew her loyalty rang true. He had considered giving Princess her phone so she could make frequent calls to her family and friends, but Princess might have been a snitch. He was almost certain cops would be at his door as soon as she was allowed to make the first unsupervised call. The rest of the girls didn't need one because their family situations were so fucked up that the house proved to be more of a family than they had ever experienced.

So Kesh it was. Mace put out his joint with the decision to grace Kesh's bedroom with his presence and announce to her that she would be staying with him for the night. As Mace bounded to the top of the steps he heard a familiar sound and stopped suddenly. Dropping all thoughts of Kesh from his mind he turned on his heels and darted back to his bedroom.

Boom!

CJ instinctively tossed Princess out of his bed and onto the floor at the alarming sound of his door being kicked in. He rolled onto the floor when Mace entered the room carrying a gun in his hand.

Pop! Pop! Pop!

"Fuck!"

The deafening roar of gunfire was immediately followed by three loud thumps as the bullets found their resting place in the wooden headboard CJ had only seconds ago been laying against. CJ tried to reach for his 9mm inside the nightstand as Princess snatched the cum stained sheet off the mattress, hastily wrapped it around her naked body, and slid under the bed. CJ knew Mace had heard hear her cries as she grinded on him and wasn't surprised those cries had gotten Mace's attention. What did surprise CJ, was Mace kicking in his door and showing up with a gun.

CJ failed to grab his weapon as Mace made his way closer to him, and put the barrel of the gun to his face. CJ stared down the barrel of Mace's gun with no fear in his heart. It wouldn't be the first time he played chicken with a shooter.

CJ said through gritted teeth, "I thought we wasn't taking bitches personal?"

"Nah," Mace said, "but I take my money very personal."

"So you gonna face your partner with a gun?"

"You breeched the contract my nigga. I need 5g's right now. I told you, you want that bitch, you pay for her."

The tension between them was raising the temperature in the room. The doorway was filling with heads peeking in trying to see what CJ's next move would be. CJ sucked his teeth as his cockiness failed to simmer.

"Well I guess your so called bottom bitch owes you some money because she came in my room looking to get crushed. Matter of fact, she was begging to sit on my lap, talking 'bout midnight motivation or some shit. The ho was out of line."

"Ho to the car or car to the ho, I need my dough. Remember that saying, homie?" Mace was taking it back, flashing lines of old time's they shared early in the pimp game. It was a creed they lived by for their business.

"Kesh!" CJ yelled, seeing Kesh's face in the bedroom's entrance. She locked eyes with CJ.

"Grab my money out my pants for Mace," CJ said calmly.

Kesh pushed past the other girls, bumping shoulders, and ran to CJ's pants tossed on the bedroom dresser. She pulled out a husky knot of hundred dollar bills and placed it in Mace's palm.

"That's like seven, my nigga," CJ said, "keep the change. I'll make it back. The rules are the rules, right?"

"Glad we understand the rules in this house, homie."

Mace stopped pointing the gun at CJ's head and tucked the pistol into his waistline, then in one swift motion reached under the bed and grabbed a hold of Princess's ankle.

It happened too fast for Princess to react or make an effort to grip the bed's frame. The screeching sound of her body rubbing against the hardwood was amplified to her own ears. Before she knew it, she was fighting Mace to keep the sheet on her bare body.

"Mace, stop!" She hoped someone would interfere but of course no one did. Mace balled up the sheet and threw it onto the bed. He put his foot onto her naked breast and pressed down so hard he left her gasping for air.

"I need 5g's right now, Princess. You don't make no money and no moves without me you understand? I've given you easy ways out so far and now you think you run shit? I run everything." Mace moved his foot to her neck line readjusting the pressure to her airway. "Now go get my money."

Mace's voice shook the house as Princess gasped for air. Mace removed his foot while tears streamed down her cheeks and onto the floor. Mentally she had prepared herself for a hard smack, but now she wasn't sure if he would keep her alive for another night. Everyone looked away as she struggled to her feet, everyone but CJ and Yani. CJ was gloating in the background and Yani was nowhere in sight.

Princess, humiliated, used her hands to wrap around her aching breast and tried to rush past Mace and out of the room. As she crossed his path, Mace clinched his fist and sent a blow to her jaw, busting her lip and breaking the skin, and causing the once juicy cushions leaked crimson blood. Princess stumbled onto the bed and Mace grabbed the back of her neck and led her out the room as the girls parted like the sea to allow their passage.

Princess was really afraid once Mace got her out of the room. "Mace, I'm sorry," she cried, anticipating another blow. "I have your money; please stop."

"Get my money, Princess," Mace wasn't the least bit weakened by her plea.

Princess, still in Mace's grasp, moved her mattress to feel for her money. Mace grabbed her arms and flung her body against the hardwood floor. She fell hard, the impact hurting her hip. Helplessly, she watched Mace flip the mattress onto the floor and began collecting every last dollar of the nine grand she saved.

"No!" Princess yelled. She struggled to her feet and stumbled towards Mace. Mace didn't even turn around. He met her with a powerful backhand to the face.

Princess landed on the floor once again. Her already bruised mouth was now pouring more blood out of the open wound. Mace hawked a big glob of spit in her face and locked Princess, lip busted and hysterical with tears, in the room.

CHAPTER SIXTEEN

Monday

Tap. Tap. Tap.

The taps on Princess's door woke her up from the slumber she had been in most of the day. Sleeping was the only way to ease through the time of the sluggish clock and her throbbing headache. The pain from her busted lip, bruised face, and hip was slowly disappearing, but she refused to look in the mirror at the swollen catastrophe.

It had been almost 24 hours since Mace had left Princess locked in her room, and her stomach was on *E*. If not for the bag of M&Ms that were in her top drawer and the bottle of water under her bed, she wouldn't have had anything to portion out during her lock in. She had tried her best to hold off from eating her small cache, hoping for a hot meal, but once 4 p.m. came, and Mace failed to let her out, she was left with no choice but to bust open the M&Ms and wash them down with the water.

Tap. Tap. Tap.

Princess eased the covers off of her curled up, aching body. She checked the clock on her nightstand; 11p.m. Who was knuckling her door? She knew it wasn't Mace. He would've simply opened the door and walked in. It had to be one of the girls. If they really cared to know what was up they would've stepped up yesterday or at least begged Mace for mercy. Did they? Hell no. They watched like fans at a gladiator match secretly hoping the bull would win. Salivating for blood as the matador dodged the beast. Nope, no loyalty with these bitches. Exactly why she always rolled with her cousin, water would never be thick enough. Not even her supposed friend Yani had been there for her support. So who the hell was at the door now? It was exactly that question that drove her out of bed and to the door.

Tap. Tap. Tap. Princess tapped in response to her unknown visitor.

"Princess," She heard Yani whisper from the other side of the bedroom door.

"Yani, where were you?" Princess said. She couldn't wait to wail off at Yani for her desertion.

"I wasn't standing around watching that shit," Yani said, "I was ready to whoop your ass myself."

Whoop my ass? Princess was thrown off course with Yani's sharp reply. Yani was just like the rest. Feeling more alone than ever Princess wanted to walk away, but the woman in her refused. Yani could get it just like anyone else. Princess never had any real friends anyway and didn't know why she thought she'd make one in a whore house.

"We got a problem, Yani?"

"Yea, we got a problem when you trying to get my cousin popped."

"Yo, wasn't nobody trying to get your cousin popped. I swear, Yani, that wasn't part of the plan, but *he was a part of it.* I told you I would get him down, and I know what I'm doing."

"You're in that shit on your own," Yani said.

"Yani, I still need your help, but if you're not down, then fine. I understand. Just remember that we both know that CJ and Mace are on opposite sides now. Business will never be the same. It can't be after Mace pulled out on CJ. All you gotta do is talk CJ into getting Mace's money and starting his own shit. Then we don't have to pay the driver or none of that. CJ will handle Mace for us. He can start his own house and any of the girls that want to be down can easily go with him. You feel me?"

There was no response.

"Yani, are you there?" When Princess got no response the second time she knew she'd wasted her breath. Yani was gone.

Tap. Tap. Tap.

Twenty minutes later, and someone was tapping at the door again. Princess sat in her chair hoping it was Mace about to enter. Palms sweaty, jaw clinched, she was preparing for either round two with Mace, or at least the foul exchange of some words. She heard the lock tumble. The door swung open wildly and Kesh appeared.

"Mace said you owe him for today's work," Kesh said.

At the sight of Kesh, Princess tightened her pony tail, and jumped to her feet like a lioness ready to pounce. The ass whooping she intended to give Kesh was long overdue. Still weak from hunger, somehow Princess found the strength to fuel her muscles.

Kesh stepped to Princess with a hard swing but missed because Princess weaved and threw a punch of her own that connected with Kesh's nose. When Kesh wiped her busted nose, she smeared blood across her face.

"Ahhhh!" Kesh screamed, charging Princess and digging her nails deep into the sides of Princess's face, adding more scars and cuts to Princess's already bruised visage.

Princess didn't back down. She continued to rain blows on Kesh's face until Kesh let go. Kesh then grabbed Princess's hair and yanked Princess halfway to the floor as she sent a punch to Princess's face.

"Stop pulling hair!" Princess yelled.

Princess grew frustrated at her inability to get a good hit in. Kesh had her in a good grip and was taking easy shots. She could feel her face growing numb from Kesh's jabs. Kesh continued to hold Princess in a lock she couldn't break from.

"Let go!" Princess heard Yani yell. She then saw Yani rush into the room, punch Kesh in the mouth, and took a hold of Kesh's hair. Now they were all engaged in a hair pulling contest with no end. "Let go, Kesh," Yani said again.

Kesh released her grip on Princess and spit blood out her mouth onto the floor.

Yani grabbed Kesh by the arm and dragged Kesh out of the room. Kesh tried to fight her off but soon gave up.

"You still owe Mace money, bitch," Kesh yelled from the hallway.

Yani slammed the door in Kesh's face and slid Princess's favorite chair in front of the door to keep it shut. Princess was pacing the room as she huffed and puffed. She was a mess. Her hair was tossed, scratches with drips of blood lined the sides of her face, and the left side of her jaw was swollen. Kesh finally got the best of her.

"He took my money," Princess said, "bitches need to die." Princess couldn't stop the tears. "I swear, Yani, if you don't want to help me at least do me one favor, and I'll handle everything else myself." Princess fell sobbing into Yani's arms, "I just want to go home."

QUIANA

CHAPTER SEVENTEEN

"We need to talk," Yani said. She took a seat next to her cousin who was oiling his gun. He looked at her as if he could read her mind.

"What's up, cuz?" CJ asked.

"Things are never going to be the same between you and Mace are they, CJ?"

CJ continued oiling his piece, then replaced the bullets in the clip one by one. The past 24 hours had been rough on his nerves and his patience was running thin. As much as he wanted to keep things kosher, the relationship between him and Mace could never be the same after Mace put a gun in his face and took money from his pockets. The decision between business and revenge was firmly at hand, and the trigger seemed like the only way to work.

"Yanika, it's over. All good things come to an end, right? It's taking every bit of strength for me not to blast that nigga's head off. I bet he think the air is clear right? Nah, shit ain't clear, at all. I just think his little Princess might get me knocked by the cops if I do it. I'm not sure how to move. Fuck it, might have to handle her too for playing with my life. I don't know, Yani, the man in me is saying take the money and roll. Me and you can go back to Alabama and start something up, take some of the girls and start a strip club."

"Pimpin' ain't easy," Yani said, "but it sure is your favorite line of work." She laughed. Then in a more serious tone said, "So just like that we're done? You think Mace is just going let you take a third of the pot and roll?"

"That nigga don't have a choice. He thinks he runs shit but he don't, we all pitched in. He got girls, I got girls. He got clients, I got clients. He lucky to be alive, Yani, he better take what he can get. You don't pull a gun on a nigga unless you prepared to shoot. That nigga really wanted my life."

"So what if we took all the money?" Yani asked.

"Cousin, what you know about robbing a nigga?"

"I know that I can get the other girls to be down with us, and I know that you can get access to the safe in Mace's room. I always wanted to know, why do y'all keep the safe in Mace's room?"

"When he bought the house that's where he got it originally installed. Me and Ro got down with him and tossed up thirds. We had you to keep the books so I wasn't worried much about no slick shit." CJ shook his head. "All the work we put in. Now it's all ending and all over a bitch." He shook his head again. "If we do this, I'll have to take him out."

"Well check this out, CJ, I have the duplicate books and the client list. I know you got your own bread, but this house safe has at least a mil. I know y'all were saving for another house. You, Ro, and Mace gotta have a couple hundred thousand a piece, maybe even more."

"You watchin my pockets, Yani?"

"Nah, I watch the house. If I got $40,000 saved, I know y'all got that at least by ten!"

"Something like that."

"Well we need that. All of that. I'll get the girls and the books. You get Mace, and make sure the limo is out front. We're so far into the desert by the time he's found we'll be on somebody's farm."

"So I'm gonna have to pop the driver too. I fuck with Julio, but I'll just escort him to an alley in the city and handle that, then meet y'all at the airport."

"Me and Princess have the driver covered."

"Princess?"

"Yes, Princess. We've been working on this plan way before you and Mace had beef. Shit, that just sped the motion for the plan. We know the driver's history. Toss him a couple stacks to get ghost and go back to Mexico. Matter of fact, I'll put up my bread."

"So you ready, huh?" CJ said.

"Riding for my cuz," She smiled.

"Oh, you don't have to tell me." CJ kissed his cousin on the top of her head then kissed his favorite gun."

Tuesday

Princess broke everything down to the girls as they listened by the pool. She explained how with or without them things were going down, and that it would be smart to pick a side and pack. At first they responded as if it was a game. But once she made it clear that CJ was her backup, everyone knew shit was real.

"I knew after the other night CJ was going to want revenge," Kitty said. "There was no way he was going to let that shit ride." Kitty went on to jokingly describe CJ's facial expressions. "But what about us, Princess, my family gotta eat. I think it's selfish to fuck up our money because of y'all personal beefs. Mace ain't never do shit to us."

All of the girls agreed with Kitty. Princess knew they would find a reason not to go. Mace was good to *them*, he was their daddy. He bought in wealthy clients, kept a roof over their heads, and food in their stomachs. He was possibly the best pimp any pimp could ever be. Those hos would starve in the wild. Princess knew she couldn't match Mace's empire. Like any smart man, he did everything for his girls, that made it hard for anyone to succeed at taking his spot. Being able to take out the king and promise the peasants food to eat, would be a lie even she couldn't mask. Back in Philly, there was no way she could keep all seven of them happy without making enemies in the process. With no real clientele, no housing, and no idea of how much startup money they'd have, all she'd be doing is hustling hope and selling dreams.

"No, Mace didn't do anything to you, but he didn't offer you anything either. Y'all come home with me and we can take Philly over. I'll give y'all a house percentage and all the perks. I'll buy the house and handle everything else, I just need you to work and help find clients. It'll be like working for yourself but paying rent. Quit whenever you want, work three weeks a month just like here. No pimps, no restrictions. Just a bunch of bad bitches getting money together. If you're not down fine, but either way, this run is done."

"So," Gigi said, "you're telling me CJ is going to let us own and run our own house as an equal? I'm not buying it." Princess had to admit to herself it did seem far-fetched. She wasn't prepared for that question.

"Nah, CJ's going back to Alabama," Princess said.

"So Yani's going with him then?" Gigi asked. "I can't see them splitting up. And he's just going to let you start some shit on his dime?"

Questions were swarming around like bees around a hive. Princess became defensive because of all the surrounding doubt.

"Do whatever you want," Princess said, "I don't have time for this. I told you what it is. The limo leaves tomorrow; don't get left behind."

QUIANA

For all she cared, those bitches could die in the desert. Too much had to be done in the next twenty four hours. They would have to see for themselves.

Wednesday, 2 AM

Mace sat on the bed and watched Kesh's pole dancing performance. He felt half dead. His conscience had been fucking with him, things were beginning to spiral out of control in his house, and needed to be checked ASAP. Drowning his emotions in Hennessey and barrels of Kush weed, had his body on tilt.

Princess was done. He couldn't deny his feelings for her, but he would have to extinguish the fire himself before he had another Lauren on his hands. Princess was unappreciative towards all he had done for her, and he'd be damned if he would be played for a fool twice in his life by a woman. She could walk the desert and die a slow death of hunger and thirst. Fucking with him meant being food for the vultures.

On top of everything the practice he preached on loyalty was now another song for the birds to sing too. CJ betrayed him. Mace just wished Ro had been back from Texas to witness it himself. Mace had the feeling blood would be shed by the time Ro was due to return in two days.

Things were too complex. If he could've changed his actions he would've, but he couldn't. He should've dealt with CJ in private. Princess, however, deserved everything she got and more. How could he have let her get the best of him? He'd let another ho fuck him over? He had been playing Russian roulette with his feelings and his profession, and that made him sick to his stomach.

The few scars on Kesh's face were nothing a little patchwork of concealer and dim bedroom lighting couldn't hide. She'd proved her loyalty to Mace when she clawed Princess's face and had been holding Mace down, sexually, in Princess's absence. Kesh had no intention on losing her place again. She held tightly onto the pole in Mace's room as she leaned her body weight to one side and gracefully spun around. She looked to Mace for his reaction to her dancing and saw that his eyes were practically shut.

Exasperated that her attempts to entice Mace were a failure, Kesh stopped gyrating her hips and gave her legs a rest. She walked over to Mace, removed the tiny roach from his fingertips and dropped it in the ashtray.

"Papi," she said, "let me take your clothes off and help you into bed." Kesh carefully guided Mace until he lay flat on the bed, then she removed his shoes and pants.

By the time she got to his shirt his eyes were all the way shut. Her hand itched signaling it was time to peel a few stacks out of Mace's pants pocket. Luckily, Mace had been on a drinking binge and she had been able to profit from every minute of it. Until she had her share of the safe, these little bonuses would have to do. She tucked the money deep into the pocket of her satin robe and cuddled next to her slumbering beast.

Princess sat in her favorite chair unable to sleep. As if her mind was a projector for her life, she had been reflecting on the past three months, the scenes repeating themselves from the time she met Mace at the bar all the way up until that very moment. Life in Philly would never be the same again after her trip to Vegas was through. She knew she would be taking a big risk, but she also knew a way to make good money now, and she had the inside knowledge on how not to get caught. She thought about her ex-boyfriend T, and how he was an early introduction to Mace at a young age. Something about her attracted controlling men who manipulated her feelings to keep her by their side; and something about her had been attracted to them. But not anymore. She had grown and witnessed more than her catholic school upbringing had ever prepared for her. Everything her parents had tried to protect her from, had happened because of her being a curious kitty.

It had been easy for her 18 year old mind to believe that some drug dealer would scoop her up for trips, shopping sprees, and cars, and paint a giant heart around their relationship like she had read in books. It was easy to imagine she would be that one in a million who unknowingly met an up and coming rapper in a club who would decide she would be the one to settle down with; or even that she would meet her a ball player and a reality show contract was on its way with other money making opportunities. Forgetting about the fact that she could be one of the many who never return home, that end up on the side of a milk carton, her life recaptured by an old high school photo, she'd chase the fantasy and ended up in the middle of the Nevada desert in an almost similar situation. No time to cry anymore. The damage had been done and milk was all over the floor. It was time to clean up.

12 PM

"Julio will be here at 9:30," CJ said. "By that time all of the clients must be out the house, so I hope you booked them correctly."

"The last client leaves at eight," Yani said, "giving Julio an hour to get to the city and an hour to return." Yani stood in CJ's bedroom, proud of how she and her cousin were working together like a Mafia. She couldn't wait to see what their future would hold in Alabama.

"The other girls should be in the limo by 9:45." CJ said. "If you can't handle getting them to move, I can light some fire in their asses; just give me the word." CJ tapped his waistline and flashed the pistol tucked in his pants.

"Everyone will be in there but Kesh. She's so up under Mace's ass she wouldn't even have a clue what to squeal if he came looking for us."

"Ain't no come looking for us," CJ said.

"So you're sure you're going to kill him?" Yani's stomach churned a bit. She felt a pinch of guilt. Soon she would be walking past a dead man for the rest of the day until it was time to leave the house. She made her mind up to stay out of his path so it wouldn't weigh on her conscience too heavily.

"Just play it cool, Yanika, and make sure the rest of the girls act normal too. Matter of fact, you shouldn't have told them nothing. With all of them involved, if the cops ever start investigating, one of them might snitch. We should've planned a night on the town and told them the deal on our way to the airport."

"You're right, I shouldn't have. But everything will be cool. I can't wait to get home, we're gonna set it on fire with our club."

"First things first, cuz. I want to let you know if things don't work out as planned, you keep living."

Yani put her head down and paused in thought. What he was saying was true. At the end of the day, there was still a risk that Mace wouldn't go down without a fight. That's why it was always important to catch the cat while he was sleeping.

"And if anything happens to me," Yani replied, "you do the same."

4PM

"You know CJ will start his own shit," Gigi said to Hannah, Kitty and the rest, "which means Ro will be down too. Yani will have to leave with him. So this dream of kicking some shit off in Philly ain't gonna happen. Plus I'm ready for some new shit anyway. I can't do this my whole life."

The crew sat and listened in Gigi's bedroom while she explained why they needed to rock out with CJ and Ro if they wanted to continue to eat and live like they had been. It was a scary thing for most of them. Being totally on their own would be hard, and a job was not an option. Their walls were about to come tumbling down, and if anyone could put them back up, they decided it would be CJ not Princess.

6PM

Muhammad stripped down to nothing but his thick course beard. The Bin Laden look alike was nothing but a 6'4" set of olive tone skin and bones underneath his heavy attire. Out of all the clients she had in the past few months, none made her feel as uncomfortable as he did. His eyes were intimidating. The way he watched her as she moved around the room made her feel as if she were being stalked. The lights were low and Yani did a good cover up job on her battle wounds, yet he was fixed on her face. His coldness raised bumps on her skin, but she still attempted to warm up the situation.

Muhammad lay on the bed with his long legs extended and spread wide, his hands tucked behind his head, and his little, 5 inch penis pointing directly at her. Muhammad was very formal and kept the conversation so short it was non-existent. Princess cringed. Back in Saudi Arabia he had four wives who had to bare his crayon sized dick on the daily. Muhammad was a hairy middle aged man with thick patches of dark hair quilting his chest, legs, back and of course penis. His beard and eyebrows were a good indication that he was indeed a hairy beast.

Princess straddled Muhammad, forcing his penis to enter her vaginal walls. His dick was half soft and could barely stay inside. Still, Princess proceeded to bounce up and down and cry out moans of enjoyment.

"Uhhh," he grunted as she turned her face away in utter irritation. Realizing that he wasn't built to last or to stay inside, she dismounted the exhausted fuck and kneeled in the between his legs to orally please him.

After ten minutes of an Oscar worthy performance Princess tempted his milk bottle with a straw suck. She gagged having to perch her lips on the head of his cock.

The Vienna sausage left room in her mouth, and felt more like an uncooked pretzel than a swirly lollipop. He continued to allow her to suck in silence. Princess kept her eyes on the digital clock wishing 10 o'clock would come.

8 PM

Yani watched Stan clean up his last dish from the night's dinner. He was an excellent cook and she was going to miss his home cooked meals. She was kicking herself for never learning any of his recipes, or even how to properly cook rice. Stan took his apron off and wiped the sweat from his wrinkled forehead. Unknown to the potbellied sixty year old chef, he had cooked his last meal.

"Stan I need to talk to you," Yanni said. "Let's walk to the limo."

"Of course, Yani."

Stan led the way to the limo where Muhammad was already inside waiting for departure. Yani stopped Stan before he opened the passenger door and took his usual seat next to Julio.

"Wait," Yani said. "Before you get in." Yani handed him a fat envelope filled with $60,000 in one hundred dollar bills. "This should cover your pay for a year."

"So I'm fired?" Stan asked.

"You did nothing wrong, and I won't explain any further. But I will say I'm going to miss your baked chicken and cornbread stuffing." Yani smiled with a wink as she patted him on the back.

Stan opened the envelope and ran his thumb over the crisp bills. He chuckled. "Maybe not a lot to some," he said, "but to a retied chef with a military pension, it's enough to put down my spoon and relax for a while."

Yani opened the passenger door for him. He embraced her. "Well thank you so much, Yanika, I wish you and the rest of the girls the best of luck."

Yani held on tight. She would truly miss his genuine personality and having a grand-pop figure around.

"Julio," Yani said, peeking into the limo, "make sure you're back here no later than 9:30."

"Si," Julio said.

Stan climbed into the front seat, slammed the door, and waved good-bye.

9:30 PM

Princess waited at the bottom of the stairs for Kesh to exit her bedroom. She quickly skipped to the next step pretending to be on her way up. Kesh rolled her eyes and bumped Princess's shoulder. Princess ignored the nudge and asked, "Where's Mace?"

"Why?"

"I need to talk to him," Princess said, "and I know you know his every move." She snickered. "Matter of fact I'll just check his room." She continued to the next step.

"You won't be checking his room," Kesh said "you should be saying your prayers; because, after you pay your debt—" Kesh shrugged her shoulders and laughed.

"Then what, Kesh?" Princess stepped to Kesh challenging her next move. It wasn't over between them, but she also had a schedule to stick to. They would have to settle things another time.

"Don't go looking for trouble." Kesh said. She turned around and proceeded to Mace's room.

10 PM

Sounds of CamRon's "Suck it or Not" played through the speakers and Kesh followed the words to the song and worked her lips on Mace's shaft. He had Princess on the mind, and as Kesh deep throated his manhood deeper and deeper, all he could do was think more intensely about Princess's betrayal. Her last night would be tonight.

While Mace was distracted, the rest of the girls piled into the limo, bags in hand. All but Princess. She hadn't acquired much in her stay, and what little she had she was eager to leave behind. Gigi, Kitty, Hannah and the rest, sulked about having to part with the bulk of their possessions. But soon CJ would come dashing out and they would be loaded with pockets full of money. A fair exchange.

With the other girls loaded into the back of the limo, Yani stood outside the car to talk to Julio.

"No more. No more." Yani shook her head at Julio trying to explain his envelope of money. "You no drive no more; si? Go to Mexico." Yani was hoping he would nod with agreement but he looked unsure about her instructions.

"Oh, si. Si. Home?" He pointed to the mansion.

Yani waved her hands no. "Su casa. Su familia."

"Ah, mi familia en Mexico?"

"Si, go. Go to Mexico you don't work here no more." Yani was thanking God for her high school Spanish classes. Julio took the money and got behind the wheel. Yani scooted over Princess's lap as Princess gently closed the limo door. With their fingers crossed, everyone waited for CJ to return.

CJ cracked the bedroom door open, glock first. Mace's eyes were closed, he was too busy enjoying Kesh's blow job to see the gun aimed at him. Kesh on the other hand, even with a mouthful of dick managed to notice him. She screamed.

"Get on the bed," CJ said to Kesh.

Mace's eyes popped open. Kesh sat at the head of the bed, knees buckled and tucked into her arms. She began crying, "Please, God, don't let me die like this."

"Caught with my pants down, huh?" Mace said.

"Shut the fuck up," CJ said. "Go to the safe." The last thing CJ needed to do was take his eyes off Mace.

"Slow down playboy," Mace said, "you don't want to do this."

"Nigga, aim to shoot. Never put a gun in a nigga's face and walk away."

Mace bent down and opened the doors of the closet's cabinet where the safe was hidden. "This is fucked up CJ we supposed to be partners." He started punching in the safe's combination. "All this over some pussy; I can't believe it." When Mace punched the last number on the code he opened the safe's door.

Pop!

From somewhere, Kesh had gotten a gun and fired it at CJ.

On instinct, CJ fired his glock and blew a hole in Mace before taking aim at Kesh and putting three bullets into her. He looked for where Kesh could've gotten the gun, and that's when he spotted the open nightstand drawer next to the bed.

It had all happened so fast. He didn't even realize he was shot until after it was all over and he felt the burning bite of the bullet lodged in his gut.

Blood began to stain the hardwood floor as CJ dropped first to his knees and then fell onto his back. CJ held his abdomen and tried to fight off the pain, but he knew he was losing too much blood. He looked over at Mace who lay sprawled out in front of the safe, shirt a crimson mess, and smiled. At least if he didn't make it, he'd gotten Mace first.

Outside the girls could hear the sound of gunfire like fireworks on the fourth of July. They all jumped out of their skin at the sound of the first blast, and held each other tight as the last four popped off. After five minutes and no CJ, Yani broke the silence.

"Oh my God, CJ!" Yani screamed. She covered her open mouth and began crying hysterically.

Princess swung the limo door open. "Stay in the car," she said. Then she ran into the house.

Crickets could be heard as she ran up the steps to Mace's room. She wasn't scared of the consquences. She knew it was her job to make sure the money was recovered and to handle CJ.

She gagged when she saw the dead, bloody bodies all over the room. Kesh, still beautiful, even in the death, lay broken and lifeless at the head of the bed; CJ, lay in front of Princess on the floor, a pool of blood slowly growing beneath him; and Mace, whose shirt was covered in blood, lay crumpled in front of the safe.

Princess took a deep breath and pushed the sight of the three bodies to the back of her mind. She then snatched four pillowcases from the pillows on the bed and headed to the safe. Stepping first around CJ's body and then Mace's, she kneeled down in front of the safe and began stuffing rubber banded stacks of money into her makeshift sacks.

Once she had the money, she got up and turned to go. Suddenly, she heard a wheezing gasp. Princess looked at CJ and was shocked when she saw the rise and fall of his chest. She looked to his face and saw he was staring at her, a pleading look in his eyes. She paused, unsure what to do. There was no way she was carrying him down to the limo. She pursed her lips and looked around the room for something to make her next task easier. Her eyes fell on the bed and an idea formed.

She yanked the sheet off the bed. Then with the sheet over her hand she went and picked up the gun that lay on the bed beside Kesh. She made her way back to CJ, stood over him, and aimed the gun at his face.

"I would never do business with you," she said, then she squeezed the trigger.

Pop!

Seeing the blood bubbling up out of the wound in CJ's face made Princess sick all over again. She dropped the weapon and sheet on the floor and vomited. She took a moment to get herself together; she wiped her eyes then looked around to make sure she hadn't forgotten anything important. That's when she remembered her cell phone. She hurried back to the safe and looked inside. Surely enough, there was her phone on the top shelf. She grabbed the phone out of the safe, threw it in one of the pillowcases with the money, and ran to the limo.

"What was that last pop?" Kitty asked Princess, eager to learn the results. Yani's head was pressed into Kitty's lap; she was still crying over her cousin.

"I had to shoot Kesh. They're all dead. Looks like CJ gave her a few holes, I just put her out of her misery." Watching Yani breakdown, Princess felt sharp pains of guilt repeatedly stab her in the heart.

Kitty nodded. Princess looked at the faces of the rest of the girls and they all seemed to accept her story too. Then Hannah asked, "Is that the money in the pillowcases?"

"Yeah," Princess said, "this is everything."

Hannah offered Princess a sad smile then yelled to the driver. "Julio, let's go."

Julio dropped the girls off at the airport. They knew that traveling with a hot million was out of the question, but they didn't want him to see where they were staying in case he was a snitch. The group decided it would be better to take sleeping shifts at the airport two at a time. In the morning they separately caught cabs to a hotel to count the money. After the money was counted, Princess gave the girls $100,000 each, giving Yani a bulk to hold for the house in Philly. They each traveled to five different banks, setting up several accounts.

179

The crew raced back to the airport with just enough time to check in. With the hugs and kisses and no sure fire way to stay in contact they said their tearful goodbyes. Princess gave her phone number to each of the girls and told them to contact her as soon as they touched down. Princess greeted the friendly woman at the counter, and counted out three stacks, "Three first class tickets to Philadelphia International please."

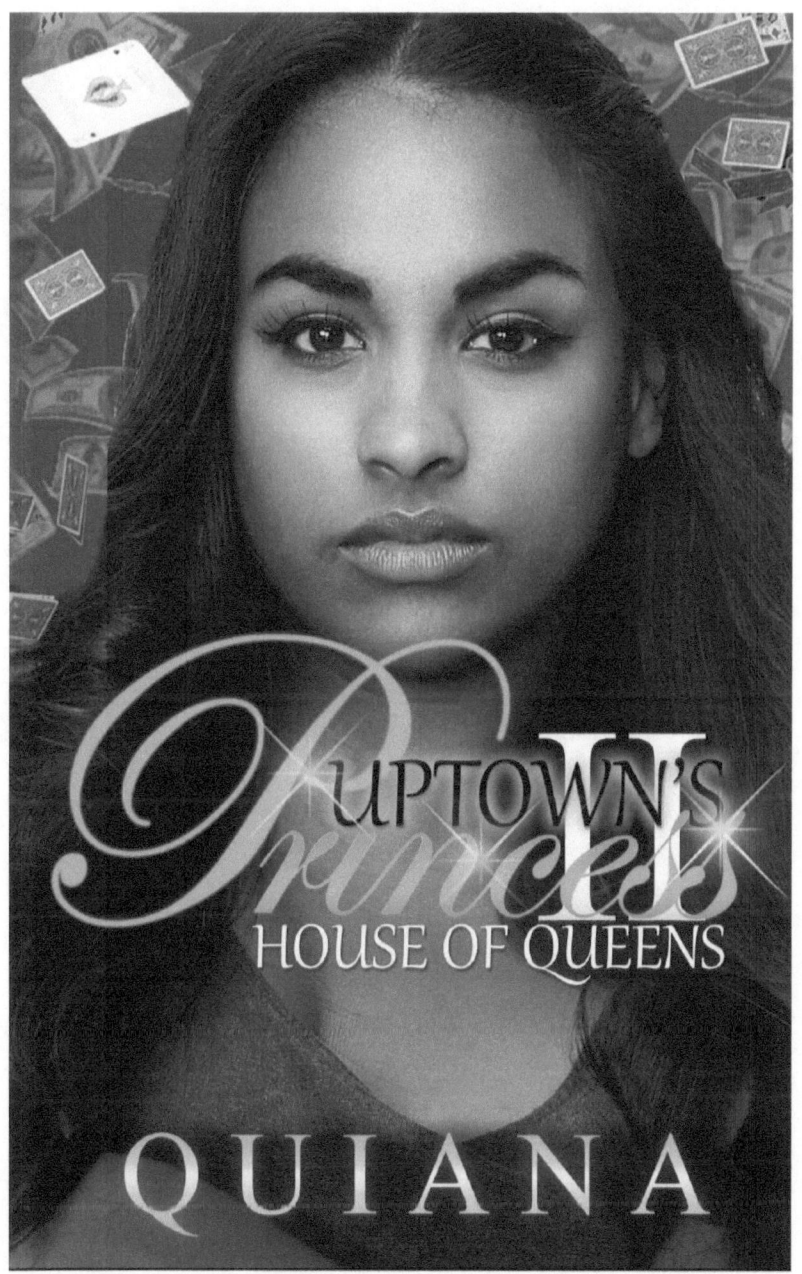

QUIANA

CHAPTER ONE

"Oh my God, I love it!" T, Princess's ex-boyfriend, removed his hands from her eyes as he grinned. Princess opened her eyes to a large stone five bedroom house, just off Green and Upsal Street. The single, corner house was perfect. It had a long front cemented path aligned with rose bushes and a large floral arch, that made it hard for neighbors to see who was entering or exiting. The house sat at least fourteen feet away from the sidewalk and only had a few steps before reaching the front door. They stepped over the humongous side yard to check out the backyard. No backyard, but there was a double garage and a long private driveway with a back entrance. T did a good job with picking out this house. She had begged him to hook her up with his friend Kweli, who owned a few properties around the city.

"Let's go back to the front, I don't want to ruin the tour of the house yet." She said. Princess grabbed his hand and tugged him towards the front door. The two entered the front door of the house, where she fell in love even more with the beautiful home. The outside was a bit classic and retro, but the inside looked modern and chic.

"Where you getting the money to buy a crib like this?" T asked.

Princess had popped up at his spot after being away for almost four months, as if they were still together and on good terms. She knew he would want to know how suddenly her pockets were running so deep. She had already prepared, and formed all kinds of white lies for her family and friends.

"I told you I met a baller out Cali," Princess said.

"Who?"

"Does it matter who?"

"Hell yeah, it matters," T said. I might be rockin that nigga's jersey one day, playing myself."

"You don't rock jerseys," Princess said, "besides it's over between us. He tossed me some bread to go peacefully. I didn't know he had a wife. But I know now, and alimony plus child support ain't no joke, neither is blackmail. And I'm not buying this house, T, I'm doing rent to own. Me and my girls, Kitty and Yani, are putting our money together."

"But why do y'all need this much space?" He said, and raised an eyebrow. "How you know them chicks anyway?"

"Cali, they model."

"Three chicks with no kids? Y'all should move in some luxury apartments, like the Towers or some other building. Even renting a three bedroom home makes sense. This is a waste of money."

Princess's nose twitched as she pushed her lips together trying to refrain her words. T was prying like any man would, but he wasn't going to get anything out of her. She puckered her lips, pressed them against his cheek, and grabbed his hand tight.

"You pay for what you want in life," she said, "this is what we want."

T fixed his dick inside his pants and starred at Princess with lustful eyes, it had been months since he had seen his baby girl. Princess's answer put his probing to rest.

"I love how big the living room is! It runs directly into the dining room like one big room, we can use it for entertaining. Yani and Kitty are going to love it!" she said. Finally Princess had found their house.

"Yea, well, I can't wait to break your bed in." T kissed the back of her neck and circled his arms around her petite waist.

Princess rolled her eyes. T was never going to see the house again. Matter of fact, she had no intentions on speaking to him after everything got squared away. She hadn't forgotten how he had treated her before she had left for Vegas. The naive days of forgive and forget were no longer on her calendar.

Breaking from his clasp, she said, "c'mon let's check out the rest of the house."

Princess followed T down to the basement. T's friend Kweli had good taste. The stairs to the basement were a well-polished wood painted black with a rich gloss, and a banister that was carefully crafted and painted with a hint of gold. There were no windows in the basement, but it was a huge room, big enough for a two bedroom apartment. The walls were freshly painted white, and there was a black bar at one end of the room. The bar was long enough to sit eight stools, and had a black mural painted behind it of the city's skyline, right above where liquor would sit.

Princess grinned. Men would flock to the basement as a getaway easily with a little decorating. Her eyes scanned the room for more features that the house offered. There was a fireplace in the basement as well and an additional room connected to the main one, which could be used as a spare bedroom.

"T this place is perfect." She said, while she spun around continued her tour.

T followed behind Princess as she briefly looked over the modern and cozy kitchen, and took a mental note to find a chef. The house had three bedrooms on the second floor and two on the third. Princess's room would definitely be on the third. She was willing to sacrifice space for peace of mind. She wanted to be as far away from the rift raft in the rest of the house. Princess counted four bathrooms, one on each floor of the house and one in the master bedroom. A lot different from the mansion, but since they weren't getting the house built, they would have to do.

Princess sashayed to the third floor to stalk out her new quarters. She could feel T's eyes burning holes in her leopard leggings, which were so tight they looked painted on. Princess looked like a Cover Girl. Her hair was pulled into a long ponytail, and she wore bright red lipstick and black thigh high boots. The sound of her heels clicked clacked and echoed as she walked through the house, which could send chills through any man's body. Looking like a biker babe in a fitted leather waist length motor jacket, the jacket gave her frame and hips, the perfect coke bottle curves. Curvier than the Lincoln Drive Highway, she was definitely something to ride on.

As soon as she reached the top of the steps, T took a nibble of her plump plum shaped bottom. "Show me where your room is." T smacked Princess's ass and gave it a few more nibbles.

"T, stop," she said. She could feel every sensation his bites.

"No," he said, "I need to feel you right now." T shoved Princess towards one of the empty bedrooms, and unzipped her leather jacket.

"Wait a minute," she said, "I'm conducting business." Their hands playfully fought over her zipper, as she attempted to look over the room.

"Girl, what you know about business?" T said, and backed her into a corner. He tickled her neck with swirls of his tongue on her collar bone. "I know you miss me."

Princess's accidentally moaned and gave her true feelings away. She paused for a moment and allowed him to entertain her senses with his tongue. T wrapped his hand around her thigh and lifted it to his waist level. He had her pressed against the house walls, standing on one leg, as his cock damn near bust through his grey Diesel jeans. Princess's body relaxed and she purred for pleasure, then she grinded her walls against the bulge building in front of his pants. Her juices began to seep through her thin tights and created a lubricant to smooth her grinding.

T whipped out one of her juicy mangos and sucked her nipple, as if it possessed the sweetest nectar any fruit could bare. Princess's lips quivered and her elevated leg shook. Her whimpers of excitement begged for more.

"Relax mama," T said. He reached into his pants and released his monster, and rubbed his serpent along the split of her vaginal entry.

"No, T," she moaned.

They were both familiar with her putting up a fight, so he continued to suck and kiss her soft skin, in between fiddling with the zipper on his hoodie. Finally, he dropped his hoodie to the ground, and exposed the numerous tattoos that covered his skin. Princess's knees buckled instantly, she loved a bad boy covered in ink.

"No, T." She said, and un-wrapped her leg from his sexy built body.

"Stop playing, Princess." T said, he gripped her thigh once again, putting it back in place, around his waist. Then he bit down harder on her neck enjoying the game.

Princess let out a sigh and whispered, "I don't fuck for free."

T pinned her arms back and fixed his focus on her face. Princess's head dropped to her chest before locking eyes with him once again. She hadn't realized what she had leaked out her mouth, but now, it was too late. Pushing her loose lips tightly together, she turned to the window. T squinted his eyes as if he was trying to read words behind her dark pupils.

"What did you just say?" He asked.

Again, this time with more confidence, she said, "I don't fuck for free."

T gave her body a light shove and released her pinned arms. Princess watched as he tucked his penis back into his jeans.

"You turn tricks now?" He said. "That's what you were doing for all that money out Cali?" He snickered.

"No."

"So what you mean you don't fuck for free?" T met his chest with hers and pressed her body against the wall.

Princess fumbled with her jacket as she tried to find the right words to say. Really, she had said exactly what she had meant. It may have been the perfect way to establish their new relationship.

"Now I know my worth that's what I'm saying." Princess said and fixed her clothing. "I'm not doing that shit for free no more. Call it what you want. Just don't call me another broke bitch."

T raised his hands and outlined her face, then formed his hands in a circle as if he was about to ring her neck.

Princess clinched her fist ready for a fight, just in case it needed to go there. He groaned and waved her off.

"Obviously," he said, "you didn't learn your worth, bitch."

T turned around and disappeared down the stairs. After all the things Princess had been through, being upset over a man calling her a bitch, was at the bottom of her list. She whipped out her cell phone to call Yani and Kitty, they were about to put their plans in motion.

www.ingramcontent.com/pod-product-compliance
Lightning Source LLC
Chambersburg PA
CBHW020437180626
46812CB00003B/1286